First published by
Austin & Macauley Publishers Ltd, 2012.

This edition published in Great Britain by
L.R. Price Publications Ltd, 2021
27 Old Gloucester Street,
London, WC1N 3AX
www.lrpricepublications.com

ISBN: 9781916467989

A RAINBOW ON THE RIVER

Concepter Bale

Dear Reader

This will not apply to everyone but because the book has such a huge message of JOY it can, for some people, be tiring to read.

This is a NORMAL and completely harmless reaction, if a little strange. If we put it away for a little while and pick it up later, we gradually get used to it.

It would be such a pity to give up reading it before the last page and miss what will be for all of us one day, A HAPPY ENDING.

P.S. To show us how to sort out this wonderful world

THE CAVALRY'S COMING..........

PROLOGUE

It is a well-known fact that Romany Gypsies have an extra kind of perception for which there could be a logical explanation. In the history of civilisation up to this last century there has always been a class system where peasantry married peasantry and educated people married partners from their own background. As we know apart from odd instances, no princess or `class' person married a peasant and with travel virtually impossible for poorer people before the railways, multi heritage or mixed race must have been the exception to the rule.

This century the system is fast changing; the class distinctions disappearing rapidly, so I believe that we will have, quite soon, people who will have a higher intelligence than ever before. Babies are being born now with backgrounds like my little grandson, who has a heritage of LATVIA, IRELAND, SCOTLAND ROMANY, PEASANT and CLASS, and with such a heredity how can these children have anything else but the edge on previous generations?

It is therefore possible that the extra bit of insight on the part of the gypsies could be attributable to the fact that a large number of Romany's were taken prisoner by the Lords of Romania and made slaves, so that many half class and half peasant babies are likely to have been born. By the time their descendants had travelled through many different countries occasionally marrying people with other backgrounds from their own, multi heritage may well have begun on a substantial scale with the Romany's but first I had to visit.

BRIGADOON

BRIGADOON is a mythical village in SCOTLAND that can only appear for one day every century. The reason being that someone (probably multi heritage) had seen that if they only lived for one day every hundred years, they would not catch the chain reaction of the evils of the period, for today, a chain reaction is what we have.

When we are unhappy others get to know - that makes them unhappy and the more unhappy we are, the more unhappy decisions we are likely to make.

English newspapers and television talk repeatedly of illness, vice and crime, and although this sometimes cannot be avoided it will often give the impression that things can only get worse. I know there are programmes of education and comfort, but once the seeds of insecurity are sown, the resulting chain reaction is inevitable because the more we concentrate on negative things the more negative they will become.

With a background of Gypsy and dress designer it stands to reason that travelling around to auctions and producing musical shows I have found the right lifestyle for my personality.

The people who run the auctions are full of fun. Laughter generates JOY so auction day must help to balance out the adverse chain reaction.

One day I bid for a box of odds and ends, it contained two lovely ornaments, someone who usually sorts the good things out had accidentally put them in the wrong box, mine being worth only a few shillings. So unusual as this crew are always very efficient. I phoned DICKIE the auctioneer but he said the ornaments were their mistake and he would compensate the owners. The ornaments, with a few more things that it had been ordained that I should come across went to another beautiful person who needed them for her shop. She gave me FORTY-FIVE pounds! My cry to God for a holiday was answered I set-off for Surrey to stay the night with a newly widowed friend before travelling on.

At my destination I found a lady who, at eighty-six years old could still come high in the glamour stakes and can tackle a game of scrabble at ten o'clock at night and win! She has too the stimulating tendency to stop people from concentrating on their aches and pains. This power is needed at her senior citizens club, I've no doubt it has been given her, along with wonderfully preserved looks to break the chain reaction of too many news bulletins and negative telly programmes that are swinging around.

She had planned to buy a SAINSBURY'S STRAWBERRY SPONGE CAKE WITH BUTTER CREAM FILLING for our tea, but she was forestalled by winning, in a raffle, a SAINSBURY STRAWBERRY SPONGE CAKE WITH BUTTER CREAM FILLING. After I had asked her for a book for my friend NATHAN who collects show business biographies, she insisted I take my smart shoes (which I had intended leaving with her) "You might need them" she said. I carried on my way to LONDON.

In the station cafe I met a lady who was single and lonely. She had the vivacity and the power to brighten up any gathering she was in, but she didn't realise her own potential so I felt it was important to point this out to her. When ERICA had gone, I felt quite worried about her and remembered that I hadn't got her address, so I went back to find her before going on to the underground train.

On the platform a young girl came up to me and said "WOULD YOU LIKE MY RUNABOUT TICKET? I COULD ONLY USE IT ONCE AND NOW I DON'T NEED IT ANY MORE".

I was on a very tight budget and if I hadn't gone back to find ERICA, I wouldn't have been in the right place at the right time. I asked the coach people for a ticket to anywhere, as far as the money would take me. My nomadic personality would be quite satisfied provided the journey was long.

On the bus I sat next to a charming young man from AFRICA who was going to university. When we arrived, I was duly escorted to a train to where an inexpensive `Bread and Breakfast' could be found, but had no success though in finding a place vacant, so I took off in a different direction. At the station I asked a lovely girl if she knew of somewhere I could stay, and she said "I DO BREAD AND BREAKFAST" (She had just returned from walking her dogs) so promptly drove us to her home where I met DANIEL who was a SCOUT LEADER. It was DANIEL'S idea to go to SCOTLAND and he told me of the tourist office where I could get details of accommodation.

The young man in the office was very helpful and I was given the address of a lady who made me so welcome in her beautiful home. Over the teacups though, I realised straight away that she was so distressed by all the sadness in the world and not a little alarmed by it, and I felt dreadfully concerned for her.

By this time it was Wednesday and only two more days left. I seemed to be driven into worrying about all the people I had met and my heart was racing with a strange inner excitement. I know now that this was nothing to be alarmed about, but hopes of a relaxing holiday were fast disappearing. The disappointment was awful, having looked forward to the first holiday for years and instead was preoccupied with the worlds misery and the poverty that the young man from AFRICA must be only too aware of heart banging like a drum, I went into a Catholic Church, never been inside one before, how light and bright it was - but wept when realising how the week was going by and how exhausted I felt.

At the tourist office a poster said...

HIGHLAND TOUR, TEN O'CLOCK.

But it was then ten-thirty. Just as I was thinking that I had missed it all, a young man came in to say that the "minibus was ready now" having had engine trouble. So I got in with five other people all travelling alone, and from different parts of the world, to be transported to the HIGHLANDS to laugh and to eat Haggis on the mountainside. Such beauty of scenery I have never seen before; the scarlet rowan berries against the clear blue sky and the sound of bagpipes filling the air. My companions were all such delightful people, who never once referred to anything that could mar our day. They were all generators of LIGHT.

We were resting in an old fashioned village inn when the young man who organised the tour asked us why we had chosen to come to SCOTLAND. Still struggling with our language, KIA from JAPAN said ……. "I HAD INSPIRATION OF QUIET JOY."

When it came to my turn I told them of the ornaments and how the many coincidences that I had been experiencing lately were something to do with LOVE and JOY, and how the fare was FORTY-FOUR pounds and I had been given FORTY FIVE.

In the evening there was a SCOTTISH CEILIDH (This is a traditional social evening with fiddles and dancing, singing and laughter). The tour young man knew that I may be short of money, so he produced a ticket and I was so thankful I had been made to take the shoes.

There I met LUDWIG, who in the course of the evening happened to remark that his homeland GERMANY had recovered faster than the conquering country because the class distinctions were absent, a pattern that later became consistently relevant.

In the night unable to sleep, the banging heart and drumming in my ears were too loud to ignore. It became imperative that I write a note and leave it for my hostess and simply had no choice, but thought, what can I write it on? Then I spotted the book I had taken for NATHAN, so I tore out the fly leaf and wrote that the coincidences were too frequent to be accident and that the extraordinary things that were happening (and I have had to condense so much) mean that nothing harmful is going to happen to this lovely world that cannot be rectified one day, only that it was time for ACTION STATIONS.

The next day I returned to NEWCASTLE and DANIEL and told him of the astonishing incidents leading up to my holiday. Just in time he saw me on to the coach for London. Settling down in the seat, thought I could have a rest and forget it all for a little while, having had my fill of unusual things, but it was not to be.

Our JOSH, a friend who had lived nearby had recently died. An explanation was beginning to dawn on me that could give BESSIE his wife, great comfort. I knew that I must write to her straight away, but what on? Immediately the bus hostess dropped two clean paper bags on the floor. I told BESSIE to look out for any unusual things; like the time daughter ELLA won the CARNIVAL BINGO, believing JOSH would try to contact her.

On my return I asked a friend, "HOW DID BESSIE GET ON AT THE CARNIVAL LAST NIGHT?" to be told that she had won the ALL OVER CUP!

A few days later I received a letter from ERICA, (coach station remember?) to say that she had had her photo taken to go into a TIME CAPSULE.

GOOD HEAVENS! Of course! Suddenly the pieces fell into place. One lovely day.......ONE PERFECT DAY IN THE HIGHLANDS OF SCOTLAND AWAY FROM THE CHAIN REACTION OF ALL THE CARES OF THE WORLD, LIKE A TIME WARP...........BRIGADOON!

In the light of the events that followed, there can be no doubt that there is an existence parallel with ours, a DREAMLIKE state where we can speak to the subconscious mind of the people like the hostess who dropped the bags, the lady who bought the cake, and the auction crew who 'slipped up' with the ornaments.

There is something different in the multi heritage mind which makes coordination more possible than in previous generations. Somehow the people in the story have, with their goodness, generated the right conditions for the people in the 'Dimension' to contact us, and have the destiny to alter the adverse CHAIN REACTION in some way.

KIA the Japanese young man showed us lovely exercise, perhaps it his job to teach it, or DANIEL may have some young person in his Scouts, who will need his encouragement to become one of the new generation to reverse this unhappy 'merry go round' we are all on. Life is eternal, we have to "do it all again" with a more evolved intelligence and when we have got ourselves organised we will save this wonderful world and literally.............'REACH FOR THE STARS'

On the day after my return from Scotland I went off

to a TRADITIONAL OLDE TYME FAYRE.

The stalls manned by people in costume with musicians and street entertainers were set against the "backdrop of the old Abbey town like some fairy tale. Halfway up the high street, displayed in a shop window rights out on its own an old TRAIN in full steam, which I have learned since, was…....THE FLYING SCOTSMAN. Underneath the caption…….....WELCOME BACK. It was weeks before I realised its significance.

That evening I noticed the quickening heart rate that I had experienced during my trip and was compelled to write. It didn't worry me in the least, although my metabolism must have been doing `double time'. Afterwards I saw that I had written a note to my friend BESSIE to say that JOSH had organised a little dog in RAY'S garden so that when she hears it yap at dusk she will think of him. He said too that she might forget him so when she hears the little dog she will be reminded.

Some time ago, RAY, who is a postman and lives next door to us and a few doors away from JOSH'S home, along with his dear ZOE, helped finance our first stage show.

He had a little Peking dog who used to yap in the garden at dusk. It was an unusual sound, she would leave a little interval between each single bark. It was as though she was answering a signal that we were unable to hear.

RAY wondered if she could hear another dog somewhere. No one minded but it used to worry him. When she died, TILLY was sorely missed as she had been with them for years and years. They replaced her with a collie thinking that she would be quieter but soon realised their mistake as she needed more room.

A few days after, on his round, RAY just happened to

meet a farmer who needed a dog and was glad to give 'BABS' a home. Within days circumstances changed in little FIDO'S life bringing him into ours and 'lo and behold' if he didn't yap IN EXACTLY THE SAME WAY AS TILLY HAD! It was a, if she had never gone.

Everyone was 'tickled pink' at poor old RAY being clobbered with it again, so we all laughed together, as FIDO is the dearest little thing as TILLY was and RAY does know now that no one minds.

On the piano was a tape recording of a performance of our first show 'CAVALCADE'. Although we did many productions afterwards, that was always for JOSH a favourite. When I reached over to get more paper, I accidentally knocked it off PLOP! It fell right into my DOGS BOWL!

Next evening my husband ALEX, an avid Radio enthusiast, was working out the locations of some of his radio contacts with his map and at the same time chanting out the names of towns in WALES that I had travelled through while on a coach trip with his Auntie, who had shortly before passed away, (or so we thought). Then he announced that he was going to cycle over to see her house (he was hoping her lovely garden hadn't been neglected I expect). I had said nothing about the towns and he was not aware of where Auntie and I had visited.

The next day I began to wonder, so being short of notepaper I took out the front page of an old book to use to write to BESSIE thinking it would make her laugh to tell her of ALEX'S trip so soon after he had been talking about the towns Auntie and I had visited.

Afterwards I noticed that I had written on the page with the caption........ 'THE WINGED HORSE'

ALEX had worn the red beret of the AIRBORNE SOLDIER in the war, and PEGASUS is the AIRBORNE emblem and his CB code name.

As everyone will know PEGASUS is a WINGED HORSE from Greek mythology.

So is his pub, called THE PEGASUS CLUB!

It was during the same week that I wrote a document explaining the theory of MISERY being the cause of adverse behaviour, my memory is hazy and I was not conscious of it until afterwards. It is the first time anything like it had happened to me and was realising without a shadow of a doubt that people don't die.

The basic theory is we have an inner capability to generate mental power. We store it like a battery does. When we are happy our positive level rises, when we miserable our positive level goes down and our negative level rises.

Now if our JOY power goes down below the halfway mark, we begin to make bad decisions or can feel unwell.

The lower our JOY level becomes, the less we are able to pull ourselves out of it, but when our positive level is well stocked up our decisions are likely to be the right ones and it is impossible to be disagreeable or selfish.

Once the battery is full negatively it has to be

discharged in some negative way, but when we are in crowds and all are happy as on NEW YEARS EVE in TRAFALGAR SQUARE for instance, the generator goes round faster because a lot of people are cheering with JOY together.

This will explain why a few people have to get into the fountains as our JOY capacity can become a bit full and the cold water gets it back to a comfortable level. Some of us haven't had enough JOY as a general thing to get used to it on a large scale and stretch our ability to contain it, so the fountains come in handy.

The trouble is that once we have discharged the battery in a negative way the ensuing misery we suffer when we realise how awful we have behaved RECHARGES THE BATTERY and off we go again. There is one big loop hole in this though and I've tried and tested it many times since learning of it. When someone is suffering from an overfull battery charge, COMPASSION on the part of someone will NEUTRALISE IT.

None of this is going to surprise anyone, but what may not be widely known, is that when a source of misery STOPS, we have a little bit left in the battery still to burn out which is like a concentrated dose. For a time, until it is all gone, we can be our own worst enemy or feel unwell for a short time.

So if we have lost someone who is dear to us then our 'Battery' will have a negative charge.

When we realise that our loved ones are safe and alive our misery charging STOPS, leaving a little left still to burn out. For a short time we can be irritable like saying something hurtful to the ones we love and afterwards think ("What made me say that our personalities in REVERSE.)

18

It is important for us to realise that there can be a lapse before the 'misery backlog' sets in this can vary according to how long we have been worrying. If we don't understand what is happening to us, we can prolong it but it goes away in no time 'if we do. And don't worry about it. There are many now who know subconsciously that we don't die so can't' suffer from BACKLOG TRAUMA as severely as others not having generated misery about it. More will be explained about this later.

So when I realised that my parents and our Darling JOSH were very much around my fears STOPPED, and instead of being deliriously happy.

I woke up one morning thoroughly out of sorts and scared, and all the OPPOSITE WAY ROUND!

Now I understand the reason, there was no cause for alarm my own GOLDEN DAY has dawned and can laugh right merrily, as the world will when its MISERY BACKLOG has run out, but that morning I was very unhappy as I did not understand why, as I do now.

I had left my motorbike at the garage, so decided to catch a bus and bring it home. Super people run the garage and thought that if I could get over there I would find friendship.

Before leaving I became unusually aware of colourful things in around the kitchen. It was a as though red, orange and green and others were shooting out at me like psychedelic colours do. The taped music that was playing seemed to synchronise and I began to associate with people who had 'left us'. I absent-mindedly took a blue ribbon from a drawer and tied it round my hair. Can you imagine anything more unlikely - being fifty-six and practically living in a crash helmet! Meanwhile the music played on.

19

With legs so shaky I had to hold the fence to stay upright, I set off down the lane.

It had been raining. In a field exactly from hedge to hedge, complete as though it was painted, a perfect RAINBOW.

When I arrived at the garage, DAVID who runs it could see that something was wrong. He said....... "COME AND HEAR MY TAPE OF DANCE MUSIC".

He and his wife DORA dance beautifully and are such lovely people and I learned that everyone involved in this experience are all kind.

Colours were still shooting out at me in the garage shop. The blue reminded me of ADELE who had left us three years before. At Christmas I had made a dolly for her little girl and had put blue flowers on a blue dolly, A thing I never do. Usually the flowers are contrasting.

On a rack for sale, was a tool of some sort. Attached to a BLUE card. There were several, the brand name TERRY, the name repeated on identical cards all along the shelf. TERRY TERRY TERRY TERRY. ADELE'S husband is named TERRY.

When the music started it consisted of all the tunes that had associations with friends who had 'left us' to join the Dimension that so many of us have not been aware of until now.

There was one odd one out though, it was ages before I remembered that it had been sung by a friend who is in the Dimension too and was responsible for producing a Carnival float, called 'THE END OF THE RAINBOW'.

It was six months after before I realised the connection between the colours and the rainbow and even longer before it dawned on me how it was done.

Also it was later that I remembered that the rainbow was where a WINDMILL had been.

On the following Sunday, the sky was flawlessly blue. Flying in circles were hundreds of seagulls and way above, exactly over my head a big plane was forging along through the centre. The effect was breath-taking in its beauty.

Long ago and far away, when I lived on the Norfolk coast a well known wildlife artist stayed with us when he was illustrating his bird books. My mother did 'bread and breakfast' and he preferred our little cottage to the posh hotel. For sometime I came across his work in all sorts of mediums, a chopping board, pictures and books, a painting in someone house, and a friend who knew him.

In the light of all that has happened since, I am sure that my mother knew that I was inevitably going to be lonely and unhappy for a short time. Aware that the thermals were going to be right for the seagulls she knew that I would be reminded of her and my childhood home when I saw them, and was able to make sure that I was in the garden hanging out the clothes to dry just at the right moment, when my young friend ALAN would be walking by, to cheer me up as he always does.

Important footnote:
        THE FOLLOWING NOTES WILL NOT APPLY TO EVERYONE.

I mention them only so as to reassure if people react as sensitively as myself. I found that in the early days of this experience when reading the book. After a couple of chapters I found I would have to put it away as it was sort of tiring. I would also have a kind of dreamy sensation, like we can have with flu or measles when we were a kid. This soon goes away once we understand that odd feelings are NORMAL. The light headedness doesn't matter once we realise what it is.

As time went on it disappeared and now have no trouble at all and can check and read the book to my heart's content.

Of course this discomfort will not apply to everyone, as there are so many books on the market now and some of us will not be too surprised.......

`It's like learning to sing. Our throats are like stiff elastic that with exercise stretch a little every time we do them until they can open up to their full potential.

So it is with our JOY capacity. We have to get used to JOY gradually until it is sort of stretched big enough to contain it. So if discomfort is felt when reading this, if one just put it away until another day the problem will gradually fade as we get used to it. It is only because we haven't understood these feelings before (and the effect of the `BACKLOG TRAUMA') that this poor old world has had to wait so long for the SUNRISE!

About this time I came across an article in a magazine about the little coastal village and mention the Wildlife and the artists who visit there. It featured too a picture of the lovely WINDMILL. It was sometime later before I realised its significance.

When I saw the big aircraft on the day of the seagulls, I was reminded of CLIFF who flew one for a well known Airline. It was three days after he died that I suddenly knew what was wrong with his son who was then in Dartmoor prison.

As English people know, Dartmoor is just about `the end of the line'. GLEN such an endearing personality, baffling magistrates and doctors alike. As a tiny boy would

22

do such colourful things. He was quite small when his grandmother lifted the lid of the piano only to find all the keys missing! (Of course he put them all back) to take him out to tea was all best forgotten.

His mother SYLVIA had been a dancer and had met CLIFF while they were both appearing in variety theatre; she as a contortion and sister act, and he as comic feed and impersonator. Half-English Half-Danish, ex-Public School and RAF BOMBER PILOT, for all that, CLIFF'S time in show business was of the highest importance.

After a couple of years, he decided to return to the AIR FORCE feeling that it would be a safer profession flying big transport planes, but the kind of personality he was must have missed the challenge and excitement that is inevitable when the entertainment world is one's living.

Being in the wrong lifestyle for our personality can develop a misery charge as everyone knows, so seven years later things went wrong for them. SYLVIA brought the children back home from Germany and bravely brought them up alone. Although she had her mother's help had to go to secretarial college to start a new career. Meanwhile GLENS little, naughtiness became more colourful and serious.

Psychiatrists knew nothing about the years of ballet training and theatrical experience or the tremendous natural talent SYLVIA has as like CLIFF she was multi talented. All they knew was that she had been married to an RAF Officer (He was a Squadron Leader) and was in the civil service.

One night three days after I had heard that CLIFF had died, I was puzzling my brains to try to work out why such an intelligent and well loved personality could be in

23

Dartmoor prison. The effect on our darling SYLVIA was beginning to tell.

I wrote to a friend who is in the prison service to say `IF ONLY WE COULD UNDERSTAND WHAT GLEN IS TRYING TO CONVEY TO US.'

Then suddenly I knew! ....

On the bottom like a postscript I wrote, "I'VE GOT IT! PRAY I'LL HAVE THE COURAGE TO TELL GLEN THE THEORY OF A LITTLE BOY WHO NEVER SAW HIS MOTHER DANCE."

I have no doubt that his father heard his sons cry, and was able to directly say the clue as that night, I could hear the word go clearly through my head; `ENTERTAINER'. He had never seen her entertain; she taught our lovely chorus girls but he was in prison then.

Had they stayed in show business for a while longer, the boy and not the little girl as one would expect, (Although like her parents, beautiful and multi talented, didn't have any problems) would have seen her rehearse and copied, and got his little act up a treat. One could say how can it be that simple? An oak tree has a very simple beginning and a child's misery can be well away at a very early age.

GLEN was entertaining the world before he could speak and misunderstood it himself, and a child's misery once charged means that it must be discharged in a negative way. Feeling guilty and ashamed of how he's carried on, RECHARGES THE BATTERY so off he'll go again, round and round getting worse and worse.

When he had the explanation for what began his vicious circle, GLEN was able to get a grip on life.

A little while after, her granddaughter sent a request

letter to a popular television programme which was picked out from 170,000 for SYLVIA to appear.

She was funny and enchanting, GLEN proudly switched on. Both he and SYLVIA have had such courage and I knew then that they would both survive to know happiness again.

CLIFF was at the WINDMILL THEATRE LONDON. At the time of writing.

It is nine years since I noticed coincidence for the first time. My daughter was working in a post office when they used to advertise with pictures of village post offices. I needed a picture to brighten up a room, so she brought an out of date one home.

It was a print of a watercolour of W--------s-----. My mother had often talked of the place. Her post office savings book was stamped S---------so I was attached to it but thought no more.

A little while after, when in a furniture store, some lovely piano music was playing. I asked the young manager where I could buy it from as it was super stuff.

He said, "ITS ME ACTUALLY" and went on to explain that he had made the recording with a famous orchestra in the hopes of getting it commercialised.

He kindly offered to make a recording of it for me and wouldn't even let me pay for the tape!

Some weeks later I heard from him to say that the original had been stolen and the recording he had made for me was the only one he had. (The record company probably had a copy but would have been costly.)

I took a sick friend out to tea one day. It was during one of my 'hard up' periods and just managed the price knowing that I would be a little short for the rest of the week.

Returning home, I found a bank note in the hedge, no one claimed it. This just covered the cost of the tea.

Then there was the time I rode over a children's crossing. The crossing keeper was well within his rights to be furious, so next day I made a written apology and changed my route to give it to him.

As I cut across country lanes to get back onto the right road, I came upon a young man who had come off his motorbike.

Then I began to notice that if one did the 'Christian thing' one would always be in the 'right place at the right time'. The pattern became so frequent that I lost count.

One day I needed a Hoover ring. The market stall lady was short of change so rather than inconvenience her with my ten pound note, I said I would call back later, On the ground further along I found one in the road.

A couple of weeks later found another a bit larger, so I picked it up. Wouldn't have bothered if I hadn't found the other one, I make DOLLIES for a shop. A little girl fell in love with one, probably because they are based on the costumes from our shows. This dolly was becoming very important to her.

I left it till the last minute confident that it would be done in time when the driving ring on my sewing machine snapped.

I rushed down to the shop where they stock the parts, but the rings were sold out. I met her DADDY who said "not to worry", but we both knew that disappointment was going to be great. Decided to get off to the sewing machine shop fourteen miles away and was donning motor bike gear when remembered the ring I had found in the road. IT FITTED FINE!

It is most important that they are totally fair, so they have to be careful how much they influence things. Nothing can come out right unless all is completely `above board'.

They know that I must find some money to get this message circulating round the world. Dental treatment clashed with a MOT test so I had a very expensive time. (Ministry of transport safely check on the bike).

One jumble morning there was, stuck out in front, a pair of tiny shoes. `donkeys' years old with buckles, it is so rare to find anything so valuable now as such things are so sought after, with a few more things to sell I just had enough to pay for both teeth and bike.

Shortly after the bike packed up, (being seventeen years old) and I developed toothache again. DAVID the super mechanic got this `Gypsy' back on the road and the Dentist sorted once more. But of course, I was back to square one.

Off jumbling the following Saturday when what did I find but ANOTHER tiny pair of shoes, same period same little pointed toes, same buckles. They were a little bit more worn, so there was an old handbag too. Instead of having to make more dollies and teddies, was able to get on with this.

I never knew my grandmother as she died before I was born, and I never knew what she looked like. A year ago, TONY a cousin had sent a photograph of her that I had never known existed. On her knee was UNCLE GEORGE TONY'S father, and by her side, my mother.

One morning I had the impulse to look at it, and what did I see peeping out from under her long skirt? A PAIR OF TINY SHOES WITH BUCKLES! My mother had said she had tiny feet size three I think.

We have a beautiful picture, embroidered by my mother. It's subject CHRIST KNOCKING AT A DOOR. Its glass was broken, so I kept it in a plastic bag for years as I couldn't afford a new frame and was unable to find a second-hand one to fit.

One day while walking down the town the day before refuse collection, opposite, a lady picked something up and put it down again.

I crossed over and saw that it was a picture. In the corner were the words, *Rowlandson, Photographers NORWICH.*

The name of the people who had owned it PARSONS.

(PARSON is an English name for an ordained minister) My brother's name is ROWLAND and I had just heard from his son to say that he was soon to be ordained into the CHRISTIAN CHURCH and we had lived near and had associations with NORWICH.

Having searched for something suitable, I think my mother simply suggested to some one's subconscious mind to throw it out and, and then got the lady to pick it up so that I would cross over to see what she had been looking at.

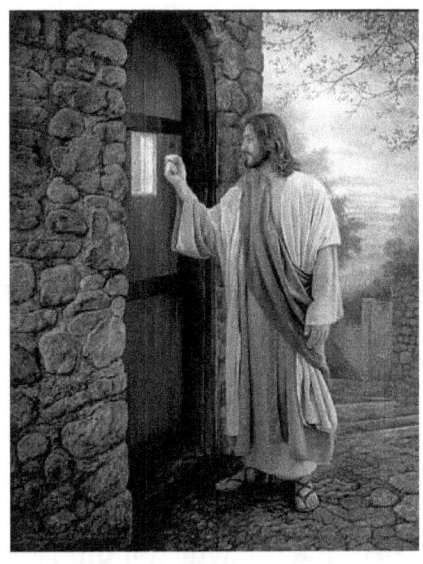

The frame fitted OF COURSE.

ALEX Came in with a brand new MUG with a rude joke on it. I had it in a corner on the piano, out of sight where it stayed forgotten.

When at a bazaar I saw lovely MUG. It looked shiny and new. And was so pretty. On it the name SYLVIA. I thought it lovely but didn't buy it because I couldn't think of anyone with that name.

I see SYLVIA often and we are such close friends and I have known her for years. It is extraordinary to forget her name.

She has lovely taste and the MUG would have looked in keeping with her tiny cottage and would have given her such pleasure. Later on realising this I unhappily tried to think of some way of getting hold of it, hoping desperately that some miracle might get it into the following Saturday jumble sale being held in the same hall. After all, some very extraordinary things were happening.

At nine o'clock I donned motor-bike gear ready to go when I couldn't find the keys. Searched everywhere getting `strung up' and distressed because SYLVIA didn't get her MUG as I had forgotten her name, and realising that `Someone' had gone to a lot of trouble to get it there. Without the keys I couldn't go. (Later found them in an old coat). I looked up at the piano hoping still that I had left them on there. Right out on its own was perched THE NAUGHTY MUG!

Knowing nothing about the mug or the lost keys, ALEX had unconsciously picked up the mug and put it down again, JUST WHERE IT WAS MEANT TO GO intending to cheer me up, which it did right merrily. She can have that one instead.

The original mug did turn up again ages after but it is another story in itself and will have to wait until another time.

When I am puzzled about something they will sometimes use an old nursery-rhyme, in which there will be a clue.

All the stories are in proper sequence but I was not sure if I had got the picture frame one in the right order. Should it have gone in before the shoes? I wondered when ALEX came in with, "I'VE CHOPPED SOME STICKS FOR SYLVIA (For her fire) THEY'RE IN THE GREENHOUSE".

Doesn't the old rhyme go;

"ONE TWO BUCKLE MY SHOE.
THREE FOUR KNOCK IN THE DOOR
FIVE SIX PICK UP STICKS".

Out one day a, friend said to me, "What was the

name of that place that only came to life for one day every hundred years?"

He had entered a quiz show the night before and had been unable to answer the question.

On returning home and switching on the television and across the screen the words, BRIGADOON BRIGADOON BRIGADOON.......

The name came up again, on tape radio and telly, during the following days.

I have another wise and sweet friend JILL who has the habit of saying "WE'RE NOT IN THE DRIVING SEAT".

Meaning to trust in GOD in things. She calls me CON as others do, but sometimes makes little adjustments like CONESTA or CONTESSA drawing attention to my name I realise now with a list she made of a lot of Christian names beginning with CON.

One day on television, a young man was teaching deaf children. He told them to 'concentrate' then mimed going to sleep and driving a car vigorously.

They guessed DREAM.

Later during a local news programme an Inspector of Police was worried about the increasing crime rate and was worried and concerned at not being able to pinpoint the cause. It struck me that he was a very sincere sort of chap. He had in the studio a row of cars, which he was using to illustrate all the different confidence tricks that had been used with them. Each one had the number plate ....CON 1 CON 2 CON 3 CON 4 I think there were five, but can't be certain as it is days before I realise the significance of these things.

I had been worried about how to circulate the MISERY CAUSES ADVERSE BEHAVIOUR document and

31

had no idea where to start. It's clear now though, there can be no doubt that this remarkable thing has happened and the people in the Dream like dimension have found a way to let us know things to our advantage.

And the message?
"CONCENTRATE, THE PEOPLE IN THE DREAM ARE IN THE DRIVING SEAT, SEND THE `MISERY CAUSES ADVERSE BEHAVIOUR DOCUMENT TO CHIEF INSPECTOR G …... (DEPUTY), I know it is astonishing, but then all new discoveries are after all, people laughed at Christopher Columbus when he said the world was round perhaps we shouldn't be too surprised that we go in circles, as the document says. After all, most things do.

To remove the fear of death from the world, will be a veritable `trump card' against the growing unhappiness that we have today. The `BACKLOG TRAUMA', if understood can shed light on things that previously have been a mystery, for instance when young people go back into detention over and over again and when things are looking good for them, will inexplicably do something adverse and not be able to explain it.

I know of a little boy who had experienced a very unhappy home. After two days of perfect happiness with his new `Foster mother' he was being put to bed when he suddenly said "I HATE YOU, YOU'RE HORRIBLE".

His new mother replied sympathetically, "DO YOU DARLING, NEVER MIND, I LOVE YOU ANYWAY".

You see there was a bit left in the battery, so he went into REVERSE, poor little love, but COMPASSION soon dispelled it. (The Foster Mother had probably looked after other children so it is possible that she had got used to the pattern of behaviour).

Now that the backlog and its effects are being explained, UNDERSTANDING WILL DAWN like BRIGADOON DID FROM THE MIST.

It is often days before it dawns on me that I am being talked to. I did improve a bit as time went on but I am still much slower than my brother would have been, I am sure that it must have been meant for him, but I'M NOT COMPLAINING'.

I have a super friend NATHAN who acted in our shows. He has a severe health problem but has such faith in GOD and trusts him so completely that he is able to stay his fabulous self and not let misery attack him as it would if he tried to handle it alone.

In personality NAT is so like ROW it is astonishing. If I close my eyes when he is speaking, it's as if is ROW himself, so NAT is as dear to me as a younger brother would be.

He comes to the auctions sometimes, which are held outside in the open air. I began to notice that when I saw him, I would shortly see a lorry with the full name of our baby brother who died before I was born on its side. It's not surprising that our name should be on the trader's lorry, as both Christian and surname are quite common but began to notice the timing and that when it passed NAT was going to be around.

He had given me a photo album with pictures of our shows, and had been responsible for the tape recording of CAVALCADE (The tape that fell into the DOGS BOWL.) I had stuck the album on the piano with the tape where I could see it, sure that it had some meaning. On the cover was a picture of a GOLDEN SKY.

I live in a simple house in a long row of council built

houses. My neighbours, all of them the most amiable and kind people one could find. In all the 35 years I have lived here I don't remember a single episode of tension or unkindness. Together too we have worked on happy projects like Carnivals and stage shows. It can be called without any exaggeration 'a happy place.'

I had given the BRIGADOON STORY to a lot of my friends to read and one by one so many of them simultaneously, became 'distant'.

This negative reaction that people can sometimes have is temporary and harmless. If we understand what it is we get over it in 'no time' but it was in the early days of this experience and I did not realise that it is made worse if a lot of people get to know at once and will then take longer to 'burn out' and some of us will go into REVERSE.

In retrospect, I am sure that It was deliberately organised as part of my education to understand this. It is all applying to a few years ago, there is a logical explanation for why the 'backlog trauma, everywhere will not be so severe now as it was then but in the beginning of this experience all was unavoidable and until it went away. I just had to wait until my darling friends came back to me as the backlog, when we realise that our consciousness is permanent is TEMPORARY. And I must point out again, does not affect everyone, I was very lonely for a time so I popped out for a bit of jumbling to try to get rid of the misery that I was in danger of generating which was like a grief and aching in my heart.

A book fell open with a picture of NOAH'S ARK with a RAINBOW REFLECTING ON THE WATER. Which triggered off the song in my mind ... YOU'VE GOT TO ACCENT THE POSITIVE (musical notes here) And the words go on to mention JONAH in the ark.

I was certainly being my own 'JONAH' with the way I was feeling, as the more we concentrate on the negative the worse it gets.

In the afternoon I went off again to another jumble sale trying to shake it off, I found a lovely picture of a CARGO JET PLANE, the airline the same as CLIFF'S and I think could be the type he flew, and a little RESCUE HELICOPTER for one of my grandsons.

When I got home, I recalled that 'CAROUSEL' the musical was advertised on the television for that day and thought that if I switched on, it would take my mind off the unhappiness. The play had just got to the point where the daughter of BILLY BIGELOW was being left out by her friends and very lonely and unable to handle it.

BILLY, a bit of a ne'er-do-well had got into bad company and died before she was born, but was able to see her and know what a pickle she had been in and eventually was able to make her understand that he was there, and comfort came with the song;

WHEN YOU WALK THROUGH A STORM HOLD YOUR HEAD UP HIGH AND DON'T BE AFRAID OF THE DARK,

And the words go on;

AT THE END OF THE STORM, THERE'S A GOLDEN SKY AND A BRIGHT SILVER SONG OF A LARK.

BILLY had come to the rescue as CLIFF had come to GLEN'S and of course, the picture of NATS'S GOLDEN SKY.

35

When I took my old dog into the field the next morning, a LARK was singing his head off and the heartache was EASED.

I must learn to do what NAT does, and just TRUST Just as I was writing up the notes for this story, ALEX switched on his tape recorder and the song:

THERE'S A RAINBOW ON THE RIVER.
THE SKIES ARE CLEARING,
YOU'LL SOON BE HEARING A HEAVENLY SONG
ALL THE DAY LONG.

While on my first trip to MRS KING, (BRIGADOON STORY) in SURREY (Whose husband JIMMY was for `donkey's years' on the railways, and has driven the LONDON TO SCOTLAND STEAM EXPRESS) The GOLDEN WEDDING CLOCK slowed down. We were baffled as it was always so accurate.

After my return at the town of the OLDE-TYME FAYRE. Another day, I saw one in a shop window all on its own. Underneath the words:

FORTY-TWO POUNDS VERY ACCURATE.

It struck me that one would take that for granted at that price. Another day I noticed more golden wedding clocks, they seemed to be all over the place the shops obsessed with them. In one shop window there were `umpteen' ticking away except for one that which had stopped. Another turned up in a box of `odds' I had bid for at the auction very damaged, like it had been knocked off a shelf. I still took no notice, even though the one in the window was identical to JIMMY'S I woke up one morning with the music CORONATION SCOT going through my head, so decided to write to MRS KING.

I mentioned the music but thought no more, A few days later I noticed there were pictures of STEAM ENGINES everywhere so I wrote off to Surrey again, saying that I was getting STEAM TRAINS for "BREAKFAST, DINNER AND TEA," I believe I had said in my previous letter how they double clues so that we can distinguish the difference between accidental coincidence.

Later in a restaurant in the ABBEY TOWN where I had seen the WELCOME BACK painting, there were double train pictures on the wall and my friend had fourteen on his wall which must have been a recent acquisition as wildlife had been his interest when I had visited him last.

I began to wonder if the GOLDEN WEDDING CLOCKS had been relevant as the trains were becoming just as numerous, both letters were POSTED, at the next auction there was a pile of RAILWAY MAGAZINES (FIFTY), on the cover of the top one a picture of a steam train with a sign in the background KINGS CROSS, I laughed and thought, there we go again then went off for a cup of tea.

When I returned DICK was just saying "RAILWAY MAGAZINES, WHAT AM I BID"? "Fifty pence SEVENTY FIVE? A POUND? GONE TO MRS B!"

I hadn't even opened my mouth and had been behind him. Everyone roared with laughter. They all know I go there for stuff for resale. What on earth was I going to do with FIFTY RAILWAY MAGAZINES? I had said nothing about the steam engines to anyone there and hadn't realised their significance anyway.

When I got home, I saw the top magazine cover had a picture of THE CORONATION SCOT, in the centre page and on the back cover?

You've guessed it? THE CORONATION SCOT for BREAKFAST, DINNER AND TEA!

A letter came one day after to say that JEANIE, my brother's wife, who lives with him in CANADA and daughter to JIMMY was in ENGLAND. It was the afternoon when I discovered it in the post-box at the gate. Earlier I had put the telly on and an advert came on for those special commemoration postage stamps Of course there was one of a STEAM TRAIN and it was the …...CORONATION SCOT

Afterwards I was always tipped off when it was time to ring MRS KING. An intercity overcoat and pictures of steam trains and references in a film to an engine driver and his ROYAL SCOT. Couldn't miss him really, they just keep going until we `catch on.'

Twice I have done what I was told and rung her and each time she had received a letter from JEANIE.

Rail enthusiasts will notice that the stamp is a picture of the `MALLARD' which was LINER and the CORONATION SCOT L M S, as I did.

I think when JIMMY was driving, they were

amalgamated into BRITISH RAIL. They both did the
Scottish run. A point to notice is that on the stamp the train
is picking up the post.

I must have been guided into the second hand trade so there would be opportunity to use things like the railway magazines and the shoes.

That it is all a long term plan, thought out `donkeys' years ago became evident as time went on. That some people's lives had to be organised around the multi heritage theory is extremely possible. It is very likely that some had to be guided to marry partners from different backgrounds in the hopes that a group of multi heritage babies could be born before their natural evolutionary time, in the hopes that one of them would be developed enough to pick up the code. (Which is what it is) Someone way back In the Dimension could see how much the world was going to need this information a generation earlier than if it had been left to evolve naturally.

My Father son of a ROMANY GYPSY and a SCOTTISH GIRL, was of a poor family living in the DOCK area of London before the First World War. He joined one of the earlier youth clubs where a famous musician VAN BEINE offered a years tuition to one boy if he could be found with the talent. My Father won it and was so talented that VAN BEINE kept up his training for four years and he became very accomplished; his standard good enough for the QUEENS HALL ORCHESTRA.

My Mother worked in a well known fashion store in Oxford Circus London as an embroiderers and was very musical as well as an artist of the first degree.

She was engaged to be married to a young man from her own world but one night he was taken ill with an

40

appendicitis and the doctor was unable to get there in time. To get over it she joined a cycling club, where she met the singing playing half Gypsy.

I don't know how true it is but I did hear that VAN BEINE was playing the intermezzo from `CAVALIERA RUSTICANA' and at the point where the music fades away he faded too and gently died. That he could be behind some of the events that touch my father's family is highly possible.

Family stories were told of narrow escapes, I can recall. A typical example was when my brother in nineteen thirty-eight, having set his heart on flying was given the wrong date for his examination and missed the opportunity to go into the ROYAL AIR FORCE. Probably there wouldn't have been enough pilots in the Dimension experienced enough in Spit fires and such to watch him so he was organised to spend time with a Coast guard friend who influenced him to go into the ROYAL NAVY where he was on B deck when the bomb hit A deck.

The explanation for why I got the code before ROW and hints on how they kept him safe came in later, To try to write it all down now would be such a pity as there isn't enough space to do ROWs story justice. Perhaps a sequel may be written some day, we shall have to see. There must have been others of course, we weren't the only ones who were being kept an eye on.

Similar things must have been happening elsewhere. The daughter of an ancestral Danish family fell in love with an entertaining personality, Not surprising if her public school son was happier in the theatre than the flight deck of his aeroplane. And the far-seeing mother of our dancing Sylvia, although recognising the talent of her little girl had no inclinations towards this herself.

Not only SYLVIA but her brother ADAM was tarred with the `multi heritage brush. Working in a bank, ADAM was unaware of his potential. If he had spent even a small amount of his time creating the laughter script material that he was so capable of I don't think he would have suffered from the illness that rendered him partially paralysed. Getting this lifestyle to suit our heredity is going to be of the highest importance in the future as we are going to have brothers and sisters with totally different mental needs. What is going to be happiness to one can mean boredom to another. A child can feel quite guilty if he (or she) is not enjoying the same things as the rest of the family.

When I realised that my own Gypsy background makes it difficult for me to stay at home for more than a few days, (the Romany's being nomadic,) I bought a motorbike and `hit' off happily to the auctions, held all over, and headaches that had tormented me for years just went away, after all wild birds don't do well in cages and a canary would succumb if it was set free.

ADAM became ill and so depressed he was crying out with loneliness. We could do nothing for him but pray.

One day he went to ring the SAMARITANS; an organisation that we can phone to save us from suicide. He accidentally rang a wrong number, the lady who answered was in a wheelchair so he talked to her instead, Later SYLVIA had a phone call from him to say that he had found such happiness, such a wonderful friend. She had chased all his misery away, the change in him was miraculous. Sadly too late to save him though, after a time he died (We will have to find a new word to describe the transition we make though as dying is not what we do) I have no doubt that ADAM is behind some of these ideas, it would be

42

impossible to mistake his style sometimes. Of course he will have a lady in a wheelchair to keep an eye on too. What a lot of work they have to do, that `Rest in peace' expression will have go, peace yes but rest no. They just haven't got the time.

One thing that is clear, these are people full of love and teaching us ... IN NO UNCERTAIN TERMS ITS POWER.

When I bid for a box of `odds', they all have to be restored to a saleable standard.

I had a little LANTERN two or three inches high filled with liqueur. I took it to the shop to be sold but it was returned as it is against the law to sell alcohol without a licence, At Christmas I was feeling very sad, It was two months since they had read the BRIGADOON STORY and I was hoping desperately that they would come round soon as I had learned by then that most people who suffer from the `backlog trauma do. I longed to tell them of the wonderful events that they had all been part of.

The LANTERN caught my eye, and was reminded of JOSH (THE LITTLE DOG STORY remember?) and the time his BESSIE and daughter ELLA took part in the panto DICK WHITTINGTON, We used, from the musical, PERCHANCE TO DREAM, the song, HIGHWAY MAN LOVE.

They both looked so beautiful dressed in long flowing cloaks and held LANTERN'S that glowed prettily against the midnight blue of the night sky.

As they were singing, JOSH touched my hand for a moment, it said it all really, he was so proud of them.

I was tempted to write a note to BESSIE but hesitated and know now that this was best.

As time went by, although it was Mother's Day and JOSH'S birthday I didn't associate it at all when my daughter-in-law turned up with what usually is my regular box of `Black Magic chocs,' instead she was holding a gorgeous orchid packed in a LANTERN LIKE holder.

Later I wondered, perhaps JOSH thought it would be

OK now to write a note to BESSIE and ELLA, but as I was afraid that I would cause distress. I resisted the temptation.

When ELLA was selling POPPIES for the armistice fund, I happened to remark that my father was shell shocked in the First World War and that I was reminded of him when I see them.

Ever since then, the colour RED has been associated with him...

It hadn't been long before, that I had told someone about the PANSIE bed he had grown when I was a little girl, and we referred to those tiny pansies that grow wild.

When I opened the Mother's Day card it was a picture, embroidered in my mother's style of PANSIES and I have a book entitled `POPPIES AND PANSIES' It looked as if the pansies and embroidery were saying, that my parents were supporting JOSH.

I resisted for hours, but later on my face started to burn, and heart rate quicken so I knew that I was being given guidance.

I wrote a little note saying "REMIND ME TO TELL YOU ABOUT A RAINBOW AND SOME STEAM ENGINES". It was a little while before I saw her again, but one day there she was. She gave me such a happy wave, all backlog gone, I do believe a little dog has yapped his way into her consciousness long ago.

I learned later, that the name of those tiny pansies is HEARTS EASE.

It is amazing how slow I have been in understanding all this. Sometimes it is days before I catch on to what is being said.

In a bakers shop I bought a cream cake and promptly dropped it on the floor. Went to buy another and found that I hadn't got quite enough money so wandering into a department store and contemplating a tiny packet of sweets when this song went through my head.

 THERE'LL NEVER BE ANOTHER YOU

Shortly after I bought some of those little boxes of cheese. At the cash desk the young lady put them in a bag and tied it up in double knots so that I couldn't get them out again, without a struggle.

Someone is trying to make me watch my health. The odd cream cake isn't going to hurt, unfortunately I could see off 'Umpteen' (Perhaps that is exaggerating a bit) but I may be the only one at present who has got as much as this together (So I thought at the time but have learned since happily, that others are noticing unusual things). Apart from the BRIGADOON STORY, I had kept few records and suddenly thought, if I should get onto the wrong side of the gauze all the efforts of a group of very clever people would be wasted, as goodness knows how long it may take to attract someone else's attention. The world in need of this

46

knowledge now So I got some money and bought a pad and pen and settled down in a cafe to get it down on paper.

I ordered a meal and chose a helping if trifle. When it came it had no cream on. It was one of those with blobs of cream all round at intervals and it was my lot to get the portion that was cream less, When I told the waitress, usually so kind and lovely, she said in no uncertain terms 'There 'wasn't any'.

I do enjoy food and felt a tiny bit peeved, but I have learned since that the Dimension people don't leave us disappointed for long.

Soon after, someone invited me to go with them to see the musical BLESS THE BRIDE and after all I DO GET RAINBOWS As I write ALEX is talking to someone about how some people have a FINGER IN EVERY PIE? What's that mean I wonder; something for sure.

This sort of thing is happening to others met a lady who had lost her son. He was only about thirty two and a twin.

He was engaged to be married. She couldn't handle it at all and became ill. And major operation was necessary.

When she was due to go home the following day, a Church representative told her "HE CAN SEE YOU".

She found this so comforting that it must have stopped her fears. That night she ran a temperature and had to stay in for a couple of days, (All figures as we become more prone to whatever our weakness is sometimes, during the time of backlog trauma which fortunately doesn't last if we understand why it is.

Since then she has been able to come to terms with her loss as much as one could.

The first time I met her was at a jumble sale. When

she told me about her son.

In amongst the bits and pieces was a MUSIC BOX. Someone knocked it and it started to play. I didn't register the tune, I wish now I had.

Over a cup of tea she told me how the girl he had loved met someone else. On her wedding day a MUSIC BOX that had been one of the presents, started to play seemingly on its own, the music theme from the film LOVE STORY, `a favourite tune of her sons. And the bride said "IT'S HIS WAY OF LETTING ME KNOW HE WANTS ME TO BE HAPPY."

They get someone to knock things as JIMMY must have done with the GOLDEN WEDDING CLOCK, Their senses are more acute than ours, must be, for my mother to judge to a second how long it is going to take for a tape recording to fall into the DOGS BOWL. Their senses are more acute than ours, must be for my mother to see the tiny words on the picture with my brothers name, (THE PICTURE FRAME STORY), as she is without her specs and JOSH may have been telling us something by thinking up the LITTLE DOG STORY as he used to have a hearing aid, Soon after meeting the lady at the jumble sale, I went to another where there was a MUSIC BOX, It played the LOVE STORY theme, but I must always wait for something more to repeat or link in case of accidental coincidence. Be blowed, in a television `soap episode' didn't have a MUSIC BOX! And guess what it played?

That's right, the LOVE STORY theme.

Other songs came up that were relevant clearly saying "HELLO MOTHER" And the song entitled; "MOTHER WHAT I DO NOW"
And the words go

YOU'RE MY FAVOURITE MOTHER THE

BEST I EVER HAD

The George Form by song goes on to include the Christian name of the young man ….and his twin brother! And another

IF YOU COULD SEE WHAT I COULD SEE WHEN

I'M CLEANING WINDOWS

The Church lady had said "HE CAN SEE YOU", this reminded me of the remark I had made before about my mother's specs, The code went on about windows afterwards, emphasising that they were "GOING TO LET THE LIGHT IN," When I was retyping this for the publisher. ALEX kept sneezing. He didn't seem able to stop until I had said "BLESS YOU" OF COURSE! `BLESS THE BRIDE'! I had forgotten to mention that half-Philippine and half English The bride was just about as mixed heritage as she could be and had no problem with backlog when she eventually read the BRIGADOON STORY.

The reference to the specs reminded me of the time I had written "THEY'VE GOT A FINGER IN EVERY PIE".

Days after, in a cafe run by the same people who had

made the cream less trifle (Actually they make wonderful trifles, that one special number it was my lot to get), there were some CHERRY CAKES. On top were stuck TWO CHERRIES poked well down like TWO EYES Again the following week the same kind of TWO EYED CAKES but this time they had SPECTACLES! without a word of a lie, SPECTACLES I TELL YOU!

What must have happened, when we put the cakes into a too hot an over, the top cooks too soon. When the underneath rises later it pushes up the cooked crust so the top has to split. As these had TWO cherries poked down, the crack had to GO ROUND THEM.

On a tee-shirt later, I saw the words. "HERE'S LOOKING AT YOU BABY"

As the waitress passed me in the cafe', (The same one who had served the trifle,) quietly singing to herself, she rested two luscious cream deserts on my table for a minute, while she changed hands to hold them more comfortably and singing quietly to herself AS TIME GOES BY. (Please put musical note here) The little song that is associated with HUMPHREY BOGART in the famous film CASABLANCA where he says, "HERE'S LOOKING AT YOU KID" But the DPS had a special reason for us to say it slightly differently, because they wanted to draw attention to the word .... BABY.

My son-in-law BEN lost his mum. She was a great lover of children and would spend a lot of her time looking after them. Fantastic when one realises that she had SIX of her own.

I met her two youngest girlies at my daughters wedding. So pretty in their furry coats.

I remember remarking on how alike they were and "were they twins?"

LINDA and BEN work so terribly hard, and aware that they both needed a break we discussed the possibility of a holiday, but they decided that it would have to wait for another year, when they would be able to afford it.

I had a strange old mint cutter in a box, such an odd shape. So decided to keep it.

When I went in the shop where I send my things to be sold, there was one on the counter exactly like it. I remarked about it but gave it no more thought.

Soon after at the auction I bid for a sewing machine, When I got home noticed that it was exactly like my own; different colour but the same model.

The next day riding down the road I saw a friend and called "HI TOM". Within a space of a few yards further along I saw another friend with the same name, and called out for the second time, "HI TOM" and laughed, but still suspected nothing, we must make allowances for accidental coincidences and the law of averages.

Early one morning a couple of days later, I was singing quietly in the kitchen (very quietly so as not to wake

the neighbours)

♪ YOU'VE GOT TO ACCENTUATE THE POSITIVE

ALEX came down from the bedroom, "That's strange" he said "I was just singing that song upstairs"

There is no way he could have heard me sing it as all the doors were closed, although he may have heard me at some other time. All the same THERE'LL BE BLUE BIRDS OVER THE WHITE CLIFFS OF DOVER, or SOUTH OF THE BORDER is more in his line so he found it curious enough to mention.

The same morning I went to see my daughter LINDA. And told her of the coincidences and made her understand that she must realise how important this material is and that if anything should happen to me she would find it in my music stool, I said that BELLE, her mother-in-law, had been close all the time.

I left her to go shopping when later in the supermarket who should I meet but LINDA with her little son, beaming faces both. Immediately I had left her house she had picked up a letter from the mat, One of those that we sometimes just throw into the recycling bin, (English people will know what I mean.) in it a FREE HOLIDAY.

On returning home I noticed a book called THE IRISH TWINS, on the side.

Next evening (and it had been a chilly day), met SYLVIA. We'd seen each other briefly at that afternoons jumble sale-and she said "YOU BOUGHT THAT FURRY

COAT THEN, LOOKS NICE"

I explained that I had had it for sometime but asked if it was identical to mine?

She replied "OH YES, EXACTLY. LIKE TWINS" SYLVIA told me once that when she and CLIFF were in the theatre, in the middle of her act, he and his partner led a DONKEY up the aisle. They had to carry on dancing in a true professional manner.

I suggested that we ought to treat all DONKEYS with suspicion.

Off to the auction soon after, TWINS all morning, TWIN BOOKS, TWIN COAL SCUTTLES, TWIN SHOES, TWIN MOTOR BIKES, TWIN PIXIES and DIKIE comes up with"

"WHAT AM I BID? GARDEN ORNAMENTS, TWIN DONKEYS!"

I had said in my letter to Mrs King, "WATCH OUT WHEN THINGS DOUBLE".

By this time it was summer. On the train on the way to the seaside, with my little grandsons, a little boy started to sing JINGLE BELLS JINGLE BELLS, JINGLE ALL THE WAY

Our little boy took up the challenge with… LITTLE DONKEY, LITTLE DONKEY, ON THE DUSTY ROAD GOT TO KEEP ON PLODDING FORWARD, WITH YOUR PRECIOUS LOAD, As everyone knows this is a CHRISTMAS CAROL that tells the story of the road to BETHLEHEM and the little DONKEY'S part in taking MARY there with her unborn baby JESUS.

After that they always saw that this little DONKEY had a CARROT to keep her going her.

The Friday after meeting LINDA I bought some pork

chops. Without intending I bought two beef burgers from a stall and won in a raffle, a bottle of wine.

Thee were a huge amount of cream cakes too, I was even allowed to eat one. Mind you, mine was a bit scanty with the cream.

On my return I found the fridge was empty and the close shave we'd had (having had no freezer then). Without the beef burgers we wouldn't have had anything for Sunday's dinner.

I was keeping notes about the coincidences by then and realised it was most important to get details right when, that Monday morning, Alex went to put on his wellington boots and lo `and behold'. There inside them were the CHOPS! They must have been knocked off the work counter and fallen into them and so were useless needless to say.

"SLOW DOWN, NEGATIVE MEAT COUNTER'
BE CAREFUL MUST GET DETAILS ACCURATE CON."

I think they were referring to my exaggeration with the CREAM CAKES and why they included the wedding clock that fell off the shelf and the one in the shop being ACCURATE, to link. (This was early days in this experience so it is likely that I missed some of the things to link, I got much better at it as the years went on, I think too that ALEX's AUNTIE (PEGASUS STORY) and BELLE could have been with me that day we found the chops. Just before this story, I had found a book, along with a copy of `THE WINGED HORSE', called `DON'T LEAVE YOUR WELLIES IN THE HOUSE, on the back of the book were EIGHT children in a row Auntie had talked about how Uncles wellies never came into the house. And was reminding me of her advice. Needless to say I wished I had taken it, On the other hand I expect she is glad that I didn't as they can use our mistakes to their advantage.

LINDA and BEN were unable to take the holiday. Meanwhile I was sure that the Dimension people would think of something. One day I went over to see them, to find that they had gone away for a few days.

Back home the current record playing `ISN'T IT ROMANTIC' And their destination? PARIS! Where else.......

The television linking with songs and records became hilarious! A typical one.........

'..........My brother was always concerned that I didn't study other languages. His efforts to teach me French were totally in vain. He made a recording of himself and JEANIE, singing a song about some FRENCH GENDARMES who were not as bright as in their jobs as we would expect them to be. It goes

 WE ARE BOLD GENDARMES

We have two friends who used to write funny scripts for our shows, Both went into the Dimension within a short time of each other the name of one was CHARLIE STREET. Anyway, there was this funny telly series about the FRENCH RESISTANCE called `ALLO ALLO'

As I was writing to my brother one day I remembered the GENDARME who speaks funny language, like BISSES instead of BUSSES and THONK instead of

THINK and it struck me suddenly that they sounded suspiciously like my TYPING MISTAKES!

I hit the wrong keys all the time (when it comes to typing I am as `Thick as two short planks) I thought "BUT THERE'S ONLY ONE GENDARME IN THE PROGRAMME" and as you will notice too that things have to link or repeat.

The following day I turned the telly on, straight away a reference was being made to the programme that SYLVIA had appeared in.

The day after we were both in the super market. I had bought some fancy tea bags for ALEX, when she said "I FEEL DROWSY, AS IF I HAD TAKEN TRANQUILLISERS"

She had been working on her little cottage and needed a good night's sleep.

She was also beginning to realise that GLENN was going to be alright, so the tiredness would have been made worse by `backlog' burning out.

The next week was the `ALLO ALLO' programme again, and SOME MORE GENDARMES HAD BEEN PARACHUTED IN.

A little lady NANCY'S size drank some drugged TEA and STOOD ON HER HEAD. SYLVIA had stood on her hands chatting away merrily whilst upside down too, in the programme she had appeared in.

Then I remembered I had asked CHARLIE STREET to write a parody on the GENDARME song. He was unable to do it because he went into the Dimension before he could, And the message? ....

"THE CODE WILL BE UP ROWS STREET" they do seem to be making use of situations that are already there as well as creating new ones.

56

One day after struggling to tidy up my terrible typewriting, I turned on the telly to relax when who should be on there but the latest offering produced by the same writer as `ALLO ALLO'.

"OH DOCTOR BEECHING"

The station master is just about to translate ETHEL'S TYPING MISTAKES, and very funny they were too.

I think they were reassuring me about the bad typewriting which does seem to be unalterable and worrying makes it worse.

In the early days of our shows, I was obsessive about including anything even remotely saucy. The word KNICKERS was definitely OUT. One day I changed the script and made them say "KNICKER BOCKERS in a twist"!

Instead of "KNICKERS"!

AND THE DIMENSION PEOPLE HAVE NEVER LET ME FORGET IT!

Along with TWO DONKEY ornaments that had been standing on the telly one afternoon, had been a local news programme item, A lady was being interviewed with a MUG OF TEA in her hand, The camera inexplicably honed down on the MUG a couple of times, It may have caught other people's eye too as it was, on the surface, an odd thing to do and had no relevance to the story it seemed to me.

The code became more decipherable with practice.

Shortly after I rang SYLVIA from the phone box, as we were not on the phone then, and said.'

"BEEN HAVING DONKEYS AND MUGS ALL DAY - YOU ALRIGHT SYLVE?"

She answered that she had been trying to get a message up to me all day to say that she had an invite to go to an evening jumble sale in some ones car and would I like a lift?

When I returned home from the evening out I put the telly on and there was this funny programme. An old lady was about to conduct a seance and was just saying……..

"IS THERE ANYONE THERE?"

The rest was so saucy I haven't got the nerve to repeat it. But I thought, no shadow of a doubt "ADAM of course.

The film would have been made before he went into the Dimension, but there was no doubt in my mind who was responsible for choosing that episode. ADAM of course, Next day when I saw her, SYLVIA said "the old lady was exactly like her mother" (Who is with ADAM)

58

"PULLING UP HER DRAWERS, JUST LIKE `NANA'
USED TO DO" And she went on to say that as she was
watching the programme and realising the similarity, the
phone rang it was her granddaughter to say...

"QUICK! PUT THE TELLY ON, THERE'S AN OLD
GIRL ON THERE, JUST LIKE NANA `PULLING UP HER
DRAWERS' JUST LIKE SHE USED TO DO"

Then I remembered, I had asked CHARLIE to write a
sketch on BOY SCOUTS but he was unable to do it as he
went into the dimension before he could do it.

It was so kind of MR DAVID CROFT to give us
permission to use this dialogue, MR JEREMY LLOYD along
with MR JIMMY PERRY (DADS ARMY) and MR RICHARD
SPEND LOVE (OH, DR BEECHING) and other hilariously
gifted people. Shared some of the writing, DAVID produced
and directed most of them.

Do writers and producers of these comedy
programmes have any idea of the extent of the far reaching
positive effect on the fate of the world? To raise people's
JOY level is the most useful thing that can contribute to
saving the whole lot.

It may be important to mention here, that only one or
two remarks are relevant, all the rest of the script writing
will be the writers own.

The Dimension certainly did make the most of these
programmes though.

MR CROFTS AUTOBIOGRAPHY is now on sale in
leading bookshops and what a wonderful read it is, but
then what else can we expect. OH! I've forgotten to include
the title, it's `YOU HAVE BEEN WATCHING' and is
published by BBC Books.

I believe others of MR CROFTS TEAM have written

books too since. I bet they can tell an interesting tale!

I got better at it but it became impossible to record all the `tip offs' that the code films, and plays that were projected at us. Not to mention the announcers, remarks and advertisements. Another nice one was when they, used that wartime resistance programme again `ALLO ALLO'.

In the afternoon, hints kept turning up to convey that RED CROSS NURSES and HOSPITALS were going to be the `in thing' for that day and to `BE PREPARED' (here come the BOY SCOUTS).

Recording it I had written RED CRISS NESSES, Anyone who has seen `ALLO ALLO' will know what I mean about the Gendarmes funny language.

In the programme there ere these two chaps dressed as NURSES, One holding a bed pan, in it a secret radio. They were in danger of being discovered talking into it by a superior, who asked them what they were doing.

So, one said of his (her) companion "SHE'sPSYCHIC. HER FRIEND DIED WHILE SHE WAS SITTING ON IT" and the other one said into the bed pan "IS THERE ANYONE THERE"

Later I learned that CLIFFS partner, who he had worked on stage with, was short-sighted ELI in `LAST OF THE SUMMER WINE' and I suspect could be one of our group who are influencing some of these programmes as he must be in the Dimension now, along with other's that CLIFF and SYLVIA knew, So his fear that a show business career would be uncertain could have been unfounded as so many of Sylvia's friends became household names.

A high proportion of our group in the Dimension must be very funny people This could explain why so much of this book is so colourful, combined with the fact that my father produced variety shows in the First World War, along with NORMAN LONG who became a well known radio comedian.

It's all going to come to light, isn't it?

GLEN Is a natural comic too, positively brilliant at making people laugh, as well as so many other attributes.

It was after I had written this, I remembered saying to a Doctor Friend of the negative television programmes.

'WHAT WE NEED IS A RESISTANCE MOVEMENT' just after I had spent a bit of time on this page, in a soap episode on the telly, a dialogue went, on the part of an airline pilot.

"IT'S JUST A GLORIFIED BUS DRIVER"

Wouldn't be conclusive on its own though.

One day when I was writing CLIFFS story, an old friend came in. Proper old country character he is. Lives over the hill with his geese and goats and gets around in wellies and overall. Actually, he is a retired FLIGHT ENGINEER FOR AN AIRLINE and he said in his broad Devon accent, "OI USED TO BE BORED STIFF JUST SITTING FOR HOURS LISTENING TO THE ENGINES"

Travelling in a bus one day and wondering if I should include this in the book when a RED WHITE AND BLUE bus came round the corner with the name of his AIRLINE on the front... they use RED WHITE AND BLUE for anything POSITIVE, This reminded me of a song that CLIFF uses when he wants to put some point to do with SYLVIA. Sung by Ethel Merman......

I GET NO KICK IN A PLANE,
FLYING TOO HIGH WITH SOME GUY IN THE SKY
IS MY IDEA OF NOTHING TO DO.......

SYLVIA was so funny, He could never have found anyone like her anywhere. About the time I was writing up the song, I found an AIR LINE JACKET. I don't know what rank it was, it had two stripes on its sleeve, I didn't buy it but laughed with Sylvie's daughter as they were beginning to notice coincidences nearly as often as I was and being as multi heritage as they were had no problem with the post traumatic reaction.

The following week we were all together, SYLVIE granddaughters as well and we had interrupted our jumbling to sit down around a big table with a huge cake.

We were such a merry crowd, Everyone there so funny, They could all wittily exchange the most comical banter to each other. I haven't got this gift of `repartee' like they have and could only be a spectator and listen. My brother could have held his own with this but I could only sit back and join in the laughter. It gave me the opportunity to see clearly how much CLIFF had missed poor lad, though.

In my records there is a lovely story about the WELLINGTON BOMBER that CLIFF had flown in the war, in the new episode of `ALLO ALLO' they capture a

WELLINGTON BOMBER and go on about WELLINGTON BOOTS as CLIFF has done before.

Looking back now I am sure that they were reminding me of the importance of accuracy with the boots but in those early days I wasn't so proficient in picking up the language than I am now.

OH DEAR! What is the world coming to, it is going to be taken over by POPPIES AND PINK KNICKERS!

I had written PINK KNOCKERS by mistake.

One day ALEX came in with TWO SHORT PLANKS of wood, (ADAM very suspect with this story) we might as well get used to it, they aren't going to go away. Not while we need their writers and people who are determined TO MAKE LAUGHTER TRIUMPH!

My father was shell shocked in the First World War, so it is he who rushes to me with compassion when my nerves go to pieces, (used to go to pieces) I found this out in the Dentists one day.

I'm not usually worried about going, the modern technology is so fast and painless now one gets used to it. But when having a 'Misery battery charge about something (and I was experiencing backlog from having my fears stopped by the Brigadoon trip') We become more prone to things that would not normally worry us. This day I was positively scared stiff although aware that my apprehension was illogical. I kept saying to myself I've been to the Dentist for forty years without worrying before, didn't think it showed though.

Passing me a young man on his way out, said emphatically "RELAX RELAX Just as the Dentist was poised with his drill, I had a feeling of irrational panic. The back ground music caught my attention.

OH MY BELOVED FATHER

And all distress vanished.

Looking back now I can see what must have happened, when we have a high degree of unhappiness, or suffering from Backlog trauma it is harder for the Dimension people to make us hear them. I think they have to have a lot of DP's at once to see us through at a time like that. (More is explained about the effect of the Backlog trauma later on in the book.)

They know that my teeth had to have attention and that the Backlog would not be burned out before the appointment so they think of external ways to comfort us, as on the day of SEAGULLS when ALAN came along at the right time. (He hadn't read the Brigadoon story so was not hampered as others had been.)

When the music came on and the Dentist crew who turned it on at the right moment may not have had any misery level and so were easier to direct, as they are a happy lot. I was suddenly aware of DADS SYMPATHY, neutralising misery which compassion does. The music must have raised my JOY level a little so that would have made it easier for them.

It was ages after before I remembered that the young man who said "RELAX RELAX" was holding a little girl, probably his own.

DAD uses the soliloquy, from

CAROUSEL MY LITTLE GIRL

and the words "MY LITTLE GIRL" when he wants to comfort me (I was a little girl when he got too ill and had to leave us), Had he understood the way a post traumatic condition works, although he could never forget the dreadfulness of those experiences that people like him went through completely, I do not think it would have been as permanent as it was ... It is only the tendency to recharge the misery with guilt, which generates negative charge that prevents our natural healing process to take over.

There's the ABBEY TOWN, the LITTLE TOWN, where the shop is where I take stuff for retail. THE BIG MARKET TOWN where the auction is, and the BOOK TOWN where I take books to sell and where I had singing lessons.

You wouldn't think I would need a change of scene with all that popping around would you? But I have inherited the nomadic genes of my GIPSY Grandfather and the need to be moving on is always present. It was sometime since my trip to SCOTLAND so all the signs were coming up.

I took the old dog for a walk but was conscious of the fact that I must keep at this and had so much else to do and getting 'strung up' about it.

Just down the road a little boy ran up to me with a POPPY in his hand, and said "HERE'S A FLOWER FOR YOU CON. RELAX ......I did.

Things were cropping up RED all over the place one morning. DAD around I thought. At the auction, noticing a box of odds that would do for resale. Later returned just in time to bid from the back to find that I had got the wrong box instead of china I found MUSIC All the old favourites including POET AND PEASANT with which my father used to make the piano rock. Some pieces I used to struggle with too. But most of them were his. I used to be lazy about learning the Italian symbols and in one book were implicit instructions written by hand. I had thrown it on to a chair where it fell open at BRAHMS 'HUNGARIAN DANCE number TEN,' but I thought it was number five that he used to rattle off like billy-o. It was sometime after before I noticed that the cover was RED.

The next morning when I was sitting in a chair with electric light on, when I could see the reflection of a RED lampshade in my mother's picture, I laughed as I sang the jumpy bit from POET AND PEASANT. The RED light seemed to dance about too. I've had that lampshade for ages but its reflection has never caught my eye before.

I Know I was sitting in a different chair and it was on the OPPOSITE side of the room to where I usually sit.

Alright Alright, I will get down to some music again one day.

As I write, a knock at the door.

Someone asking if I can sing for a charity evening.

My brother has a most beautiful smile the resemblance to the film star TYRONE POWER positively uncanny.

Just after my quandary about the music, a film came on with him playing the piano in his naval uniform, the lovely smile flashing towards the camera, as ROW's does in a photo we have of him.

And the piece was suspiciously like the one my father used to play. (I think it was LISTZ No 7) As soon as I had written it down a film came on and the dialogue went, while someone was looking at old photos.....

"THEIR SMILES DON'T CHANGE DO THEY?"

I didn't get down to CHECKING A RECORDING OF LISTZ's No seven for several days after this. By then I was a little afraid that I may not have remembered the tune correctly, as we had no video then and accuracy is vital immediately I had typed this a film entitled 'ANCHORS AWEIGH' with EIGHTEEN GRAND PIANOS SEVENTEEN played by young people and children. The music most definitely A HUNGARIAN RHAPSODY.

At this point I disturbed something with the typewriting ribbon and the words came out in RED lettering. I know I know, RELAX.

I think my father is saying that any HUNGARIAN DANCE OR RHAPSODY should be associated with him.

After this, wearing a RED shirt and a RED scarf to match I set off for the auction happily singing the song PLAY GYPSY PLAY

I bid for some music and the auctioneer said GONE TO THE LADY IN RED" and repeated the same words with the next lot I bid for.

On leaving I heard a shout from a friend "where did you get that scarf? I need one for my musical act' I Said What's the song he replied" PLAY GYPSY PLAY!

When the book was complete I was satisfied with its continuity and comfortable about Its length but it was so untidy I never learned to type properly so I was faced with the prospect of making it less disreputable the thought alarmed me dreadfully I couldn't see how earth I would be able to improve it, as I make the same mistakes all over again when retyping.

I was sitting, trying not to panic when ALEX turned on the radio. BRAHMS HUNGARIAN DANCE no. FIVE was playing (in the RED book) of course it was lovely but the music changed to GYPSY LOVE and PLAY GYPSY PLAY before I began to connect it, followed up with the INTERMETZO from CAVALIERA RUSTICANA, so soothing.

I made alterations that improved it quite a bit and went to put it away. From out of the envelope fell ..... A BRIGHT RED RIBBON

I must have put it there to mark a place at sometime. At the same time a kind neighbour interrupted me with a gift of POPPY SEED CRISP BREAD.

OH DEAR Who is going to believe me? Sooner or later EVERYONE I think As time went by, I realised that I was never going to completely master the typing so I toyed with the idea that I may be able to find someone to help me. But way back then the book content would been to traumatic for just anyone to be able to type.

I hit on the idea to try to find someone who was already aware of the Dimension people, so I contacted the local Psychic society, who so kindly found someone who is half Polish and half English and had no problem with backlog trauma.

Thank you, thank you, dear lovely girl for all your time and skill, which you gave lovingly with no thought of reward.

Like the proverbial BLUE BIRD, you flew in and saved me.

If anyone has ever suffered from the distress of a panic attack. Some of the following chapter will be meaningless, but if one is unfortunate enough to have experienced this – and Agoraphobia could come into the same category, then the following narrative could be invaluable.

It's a pity I have had to abbreviate so much but all the same it's surprising how much we can learn from a little tuition.

While out on the bike one day, having been on the road for half an hour, I suddenly felt a dreadful attack of insecurity and depression. I know now that the cause was only backlog having been at home for some time which for me always generates negative charge. As soon as my journey is well away, the misery that has generated if I can't get out STOPS and so the negative charge has to burn out.

Alarmed, I shouted HELP! Before I knew what had happened, I had taken a wrong turning and had to go a long way round to get back to my usual route. Of course, The change of scene helped to quicken up recovery because seeing different places raises my JOY LEVEL. Its gone in a short time especially now that I understand that backlog burn out is all it is. At one time I used to catch the next bus home not realising that the feeling of exhaustion was perfectly normal and most of all TEMPORARY

We can see how important it is for us to get the hang of, as it is the key to so many situations that could be relieved by us understanding it.

I noticed as time passed that the bigger the misery

level the longer the gap before it manifested itself. When I have had to stay at home for a long period, in the past, the backlog has not come on until he day after. On the day of the motorbike the horrid feeling came on half an hour after I had left the house having only been stuck at home for days. If it had been weeks it might not have come on until the next day or even the day after that.

Although understanding that there is generally a gap before the backlog unpleasantness attacks us. I do know a friend who experiences this before she leaves the house after being confined, so there may be individual differences according to the strength of our misery and we must bear in mind that we can get another dose later, This is much milder though and more likely to be non-existent if we fully understand it because although it is very uncomfortable we don't get alarmed.

The form our backlog takes will vary with different people If we have been worrying about something and then the anxiety is relieved.

It wouldn't be difficult to work out what our tendencies are and once we understand the backlog principal, our comfort is that it is TEMPORARY and will burn out, and henceforth we will not recharge it with worry. It's not surprising that his has not been generally understood before although I think that Doctors are on to it. I believe the term they use is POST TRAUMATIC DISORDER

Of course with such things people may need a medical check, but even though they feel so awful, it is highly possible that nothing physical will be wrong.

At the beginning of this experience, I found that excitement caused indigestion pain, Aniseed and charcoal

71

from the health food shop soon worked in my case for the, over activity that so much JOY can cause, Our doctor would advise us about this He may have to resort to some himself Bless Him when this new understanding of the Dimension people comes.

Sometime when retiring after years and years of work, it can be a little time before the JOY and freedom can be appreciated or a young mother who may have had a difficult confinement cannot understand why she seems to have no happiness in her baby Often she is not able to tell anyone. This can be severe and must be the worst one for recharging the battery with guilt.

Sometimes the answers to distressing problems can be shatteringly simple. It disappears quickly once we understand what is happening to us and normal feelings return after the misery charge has burned out.

Shortly after I had written this, in a television interview a young mother described a feeling of BEREAVEMENT after she had given birth to her baby, which backed up the OPPOSITE way round theory or fact rather.

There could even be a link with overweight If we have been seriously overweight for many years it can be a subconscious worry Its a well known fact that after dieting successfully for a little while the very moment that we realise that the diet is working an overwhelming need to eat something wrong and spoil the whole thing is very common, because our misery has STOPPED.

Once we understand that this reversal is normal and will be only TEMPORARY, the negative will burn out and the ability will return to master the problem and will not recharge once we understand it.

It has been known for the gap between a worry stopping to be much longer before the negative comes on the important thing is to understand our own personal tendencies. The more we do, the quicker it will be to understand the problem.

I can judge almost to the nearest hour how long a backlog will take to manifest itself. So, whenever I have been worrying about anything for a time and the worry has resolved I leave the bike at home and catch a bus until it's all gone as I may not drive as well. I have a raised blood pressure too at times like these for about an, hour even less it returns to normal - the pattern always the same so I don't recharge it with fear

Of course, the time will come when we don't have really serious misery levels but for the moment we can see ourselves through quite efficiently until that day arrives.

On the first day sent the original notes to a publisher, after returning home from the Post Office, I turned the telly on and a film about to start entitled TWO YEARS BEFORE THE MAST

My mother used to talk of it and was a favourite of hers, As most people know it is a story of a struggle to get a book published. I was relieved to see that after some effort they were successful and it closed with a SHIP IN FULL SALE, gliding confidently into the future. Just after this an advert for a film with CARY GRANT called SINGAPORE LADY I had sent a copy of the manuscript to my brother in CANADA He spent a long period in SINGAPORE while in the NAVY and, that was before returning to England to serve as instructor at the same Naval school, where as a boy had helped man SAILING SHIPS, climbed a CEREMONIAL MAST and later was stationed in an old country house

where he (of the scientific mind) wrote home to tell of
GHOSTS

My training in noticing the Dimension code had to be
a gradual process though as I am only able to assimilate a
little at a time, not being quick to pick things up easy. It's an
apprenticeship like in TWO YEARS BEFORE THE MAST

After I had typed this, put the telly on for a break:
POP EYE and A SHIP IN FULL SAIL about to say ......

"YER SAILS NEED TRIMMIN A BIT"

Thy don't want me to get carried away?

So dutifully cut some out and thinking will have to
watch out for confirmation that I've got it right never
having written a book before so could they think of some
way to direct me?

In the garden I noticed a lot of CONVOLVULUS - a
climbing plant which grows wild but is very pretty. As I
hadn't been in the garden for ages it was even climbing
around ALEX's radio aerial. I saw the sweet peas were stuck
with it so got some scissors and had to cut the things away.
Such a shame as they were so pretty but were choking the
flowers.

The stories all have so many clues that can't be
recorded. To try to write them all down would over crowd
them so I've been told by way of a book called SIMPLE
PRUNING to be careful not to overload the lot. 'They have
since hastened to say "THEY AREN'T COMPLAINING.

Have a Dear friend ANNA. Known her since we
were teenagers. Divorced many years before, hadn't seen
AL since although her boys go over to see him sometimes.

Her son's wedding day due all great joy except for
the meeting again after so long, hung over her head like the
'sword of Damocles: Off she went to the BOOK TOWN to

74

get a wedding present, feeling her happiness could be dulled by how she would handle it.

She arrived too early to catch the bus back so had to wait in the bus station cafe and who do you think had decided to have a cup of tea? you've guessed it? There AL was as large as life so together they waited for the bus. What a lovely matter they had, all embarrassment gone, and what a smashing wedding it was …..

My brother was due to visit me from CANADA with his devoted and beautiful JEANIE. As right as nine pence they are he knew immediately when he met her and in his own words "I'VE FOUND HER, THIS IS IT" and it was.

The Sunday before his visit a film on CANADA, NIAGARA FALLS The road I had travelled along with him with him on the way to the falls many years ago; The hotel where he took me to a banquet and the places where JEANIE and I went. In fact a right old Memory Lane. The musical ROSE MARIE as well which everyone knows is about the CANADIAN MOUNTIES. ROW like NAT can be very funny. He had signed his first letter to us after he had gone to live in CANADA when leaving the Royal navy ROW OF THE MOUNTIES.

I used to be reminded of the little flower SPEEDWELL and have remarked that it reminds me of her Blue Eyes. I found a Christmas magazine with ideas for a little theatre and a pantomime picture of FAIRY SPEEDWELL and underneath were the words "ON WITH THE SHOW" meaning this book. A couple of days later, before ROW came to stay, when preparing dinner, I found a little weed in the spinach and for some reason, put it in a little vase on the kitchen window sill.

When he arrived, I noticed the tired lines around is

75

eyes and knew that the news I had posted to him about the coincidences had made him a bit shattered.

That evening I knew of the strain he was trying to hide JEANIE too being the daughter of the engine driver behind the CORONATION SCOT STORY. The reaction isn't serious as in time it does wear off, but it must have been a shock to realise that Jimmy can still influence stories of a steam train.

Just before they came ANNA had said as she caught sight of my mother's picture (Of JESUS) "IT COMFORTS ME" .....

As we were going to bed both of them noticed the picture and stood looking at it in silence. I remembered Anna's remark about the comfort and I think they felt it too.

At dinner the waitress turned out to be the lovely friend who had been the first to read the BRIGADOON STORY. I was relieved to see that she was very much recovered and we had extra helpings of everything.

When the time came for us to say goodbye we were standing in front of the picture suddenly the lines left ROWs face, as it dawned on him that the poor boys who went down with HMS BARHAM didn't stay in the cold sea after all and the fear that he will one day have to be parted from his beloved JEANIE was gone. I held him close, realising that the backlog, like a candle, was all burned out. Clutching the pile of Railway Magazines and with the TYRONE POWER smile restored he said goodbye.

Immediately they were gone I glanced at the piano, RON and JEANIE had been playing, and had left propped up a piece of music: a selection from PERCHANCE TO DREAM. In it a song that my mother uses when I need comfort

♪ WE'LL GATHER LILACS ♪

This is a musical that tells the story of a couple who came back in different lifetimes to meet too late, but they find each other in the end. When IVOR NOVELLO wrote the music to that story he must have been inspired by the people in the Dimension. Lying on the floor was a tiny card with a design of LILACS. JEANIE must have dropped it while; looking at photos. It was from my own wedding and lovingly written on from ANNA.

I went to prepare dinner when I noticed the little weed in the vase, it had formed a perfect little speedwell. Turning the tape recorder on, The song came up...

♪ I DREAM OF JEANIE WITH THE LIGHT BROWN HAIR ♪

I recalled that she had changed her hair colouring. The pretty light brown shade was the first thing I saw when she came in.

I had bid for an old BANJO for NAT to restore: Be Blowed if ROW hadn't said JEANIE bought me an old BANJO for my birthday "Of course! everyone knows that the composer who wrote JEANIE WITH THE LIGHT BROWN HAIR was STEVEN FOSTER who also wrote minstrel songs like A BANJO ON MY KNEE, so when these came up On the radio or on records I look out for news of

77

ROW and JEANIE.

Soon after ALEX came in playing on his own tape recorder the theme from LOVE STORY. I said not recognising it straight away …

"THAT'S NICE WHAT IS IT"?

He replied, blissfully unaware of what he is part of he answered "SOMETHING TO DO WITH A RAINBOW" And the document goes.....

""2OOO YEARS AGO A STABLE AND A STAR WERE CHOSEN FOR THE GREAT PRODUCERS STAGE. BUT THE VISION OF MUSICIANS AND WRITERS OF FAIRY TALES AND SONGS WITH WHICH HE CHOSE TO WORK. SO AS TO BE ABLE TO TELL US THAT LIFE IS SUPPOSED TO BE A FAIRY TALE WHERE WE MEET OUR RIGHT PERSON AND WHEN THIS SECTION OF LIFE IS FINISHED WE WAIT FOR HIM OR HER, AND THEN OFF WE GO AGAIN WITH THE KNOWLEDGE THAT IF WE LIVE WITH CHRIST'S PRINCIPLES WE WILL ALWAYS BE IN THE RIGHT PLACE AT THE RIGHT TIME............

ALEX came home with another more reliable motor bike. The great day dawned when I was able to ride around the coast for a holiday. Its logical that spending so much time making costumes and scenery that before I found the auctions, I couldn't earn money. Although ALEX is generous and kind, my budget wouldn't stand up to any luxury.

A few minutes before I left, ANNA came in holding a five pound note and insisted I take it for some little treat.

On my arrival, it was ten minutes past five. I rushed up to the town and booked a seat for the theatre, there was only one left, the cost FOUR FIFTY, and the show?

PERCHANCE TO DREAM

Sometime ago in my early motorcycling days I was given an old flying suit. It must have been used in the thirties or even earlier. Wore it until it fell to pieces and it's only lately that I have realised that it must have been a collectors item.

When flying around on the bike I had often thought that when I write to ROW I must write Love from AMY JOHNSON, I don't think I ever did though, so that could be one that misfired on the DP's part. Not long after this. I came across a book entitled "THEY FLEW ALONE this told the stories of pioneers in long distance flight among them the story of AMY JOHNSON, who was the first woman to fly solo across the world. In it a photo of AMY wearing an identical suit to the one I was given.

As time went on, I realised that the Dimension people wanted me to keep quiet about this book. It cost a tremendous amount of money to send it around to publishers, (by our standards anyway) but was unable to ask my family for help. There is no way they would have allowed me to be short of money if they had known. ALEX did know that I am writing but I had learned, even with him to keep it a low profile then. Like AMY I had to be prepared to FLY ALONE (Happily this is no longer the case).

While sitting with this page before me my son "breezed in with an offer to pay for a theatre trip for ALEX and myself and then "breezed out" again with the remark "CAN'T STOP, THIS IS ONLY A FLYING VISIT"

When the bike eventually packed up, LINDA and BOB turned up with a bright red new one.

Oh Dear, They will have to know the whole story one day, I KNOW, I KNOW, RELAX.......

At one Saturday jumble sale I picked up a leaflet about an archaeological site and the same time a book illustrated by the WILDLIFE artist who stayed with us when I was a child. My cousins wife SHEILA has written a lovely book on CONSERVATION with the same title as the leaflet, so I embarked on my first attempt at fortune telling by expecting a letter from her.

It didn't come until the following Wednesday, but the date inside the letter was three days before, so it must have been left on the side, giving someone in the Dimension time to look for something to get into the jumble sale, or what is possible they already knew about the leaflet and book and so organised the letter accordingly.

Just as I was writing down the incident, ALEX came in playing a recording of a conversation with SHEILA and TONY. So that's how some fortune telling is done?

A little while after, I tore from a book a picture of a KINGFISHER and left it on mantle piece to frame. A letter came shortly after from SHEILA to say that she and TONY were coming on a visit. It was written on a "RNSC CONSERVATION TRUST card, The picture on the front a KINGFISHER Underneath it the words of a POEM which referred to a rainbow.

It would be the first time I had seen them since I had sent the BRIGADOON story so I was a little apprehensive as when it is read we sometimes can't be our normal cheery selves for a little while Our little GRANDSONS were with us at the time so before my cousins arrival I decided to take

them out to see a pony in the lane where I had been given
the POPPY by the little boy Earlier that day ALEX had
brought in some POPPY SEED HEADS and left them on the
table where our little boy must have seen them.

As we walked down the lane he spotted two Poppy's
in the hedge and said.....
"LOOK NANNY, DON'T YOU THINK WE OUGHT TO
TAKE THOSE Poppy's HOME TO GRANDPA?
DAD SAYING RELAX, so I stopped worrying ...

We had a lovely visit - but then my cousin TONY and
SHEILA too could be multi heritage after all I later found
the whole poem about the KINGFISHER in a book by
ARTHUR MEE, and was reminded of the ARTHUR MEE
quite valuable books I came across when very hard up once.
At the same time I found one by CHARLES DICKENS THE
LIFE OF OUR LORD. I put it on my pillow, intending to
take it down stairs and had forgotten to. On going to bed it
was still there so I opened it On the first page was pictured
a little girl kneeling by her bed saying her prayers. Over her
head an angel like motherly figure watching over her, and
in the corner is the name of the illustrator; MEE.

There's no doubt they listen to our conversations and
remember things long after we have forgotten them and
there is a possibility that a lot of little incidents are a lead up
to something spectacular. Occasionally though their plans
misfire. An example was when I found one afternoon that I
had picked up three books entitled ....

JUST THE VERY THING, LONDON BUSES AND A
GUIDE TO LONDON

The bus book and the guide were very old. With the
buses I was delighted to see a picture of a store in OXFORD
CIRCUS (PETER ROBINSON'S) in LONDON where my

Mother did her training. It was taken before her time, the name clear above the window. On another page a photo in which the name of the store was masked by the bus but taken at the same time as my mother had worked there. I was curious to know if the dresses in the window may have been some she had had a hand in. (She used to design the embroidery to go on them) The bus said LADBROKE GROVE so I was curious to find out if the shop was hers She used to talk of the buses often and say that she had to tip her hat sideways to get in as the "titfers" of those days belonged to a more roomy world. (Titfers? Cockney slang for HAT).

The next day I saw a pile of books on LONDON, they were very old so I thought they would make a good price and made no attempt to get them. They were a perfect set and would have given me more info about LONDON The bidding went up to a POUND! And I stood there and let them go.

There is an explanation though; just before the book sale I realised that my Darling friends were over their post traumatic state, and back to their wonderful selves again (Backlogs? When for a short time we will think TEMPORARILY in REVERSE) More is explained about this later on in the book.

So my own misery charging Stopped and of course then had backlog To burn out too from the relief of worrying about them all which took the guise of feeling exhausted for a short time - so was not able to respond to the Dimension tip off to buy the books.

If people can be sympathetic when we are in the backlog state - which I know is sometimes not easy as we can be quite disagreeable and our own worst enemy, it will

disappear more rapidly which goes to show THE POWER
OF COMPASSION.

JILL used the expression WE'RE NOT IN THE
DRIVING SEAT again. The next day I didn't Have enough
money to go to my usual auction but found amazingly, a
few old clothes I didn't know I had. I take antique clothes to
the BOOK TOWN so had no choice but to go that way
instead.

In the street I was handed a leaflet entitled THE
INCOMPARABLE CHRIST In it a reference to my mothers
picture, BEHOLD I STAND AT THE DOOR AND KNOCK.
IF ANY MAN HEARS MY VOICE AND OPENS THE
DOOR I WILL COME TO HIM.

Of course I thought it could be an accident, but if it
was meant for me then the trouble which must have been
gone to must indicate its importance. The DP's work as a
team so someone will have to find a publisher of religious
texts and get them to chose those words.

They set up the books and when it failed they
reminded me of the antique clothes so that I would still
have to make that journey that way being short of money
for the other auction I wondered if my mother was pointing
out that I hadn't given her picture the right title but it is
unlikely, as she is aware of the importance of getting on
with this and would not want me to waste time. So I was
puzzled.

There I met ALEX's nephew, Hadn't seen him for
years accompanied by his talented little boy who had just
passed his music exam. Written across his tee-shirt was the
name of his band in which he was playing. In the Post
Office I scooped up some bits of paper, having written
something at the desk, to leave it tidy. When I got home

found it was an advertisement for MUSICAL INSTRUMENTS afterwards remembering that everywhere I had gone that day people held the door for me, in the stores and the Post Office.

Then the penny dropped! It was It was the town where I had VOICE training "IF ANY MAN HEAR MY VOICE AND OPEN THE DOOR I WILL COME TO HIM"

I recalled shortly before it had been the BOOK TOWN where a young man had come out of a shop with the name STOKES on his overall and someone had left a plastic bag with the name STOKES advertising it. In the cafe and on the pavement a sign advertising STOKES ... gosh! Something marvellous Why haven't I thought of this before? Everyone knows of the famous medium DORIS STOKES who appeared on Australian television and Canadian radio. She would have conversations with the people in the Dimension and has written five books all with VOICES in the title.

She was often able to prove to the world that she was genuine and wouldn't have been invited a second time if she hadn't been. DORIS used to be able to see them too, although I wonder if they were able to suggest to her subconscious "I AM WEARING A BLUE DRESS" and kind of paint a picture in her mind sort of thing? What a good job they made of it too. All same the conversations are real as the Dimension people were able to identify themselves to their loved ones In her books DORIS talks of her father and how he liked auctions I leaned later that he was of ROMANY descent the fortune tellers (the accurate ones) were MULTI heritage has been noticed before so what has given me the absolute JOY is WE ARE ALL SUPPOSED TO BE LIKE DORIS. That the normal thing is for every one to be able to hear their loved ones in the Dimension.

The class distinctions and our tendency to only marry our own kind got held up in its evolution so it couldn't develop fully and As we all know ROMANY GYPSY'S shared our ways to only marry their own kind too, but being taken prisoners by the Lords of ROMANIA and made slaves when it is likely that half class and half peasant babies would have been born, they must have had a head start. By the time they had travelled through so many different countries occasionally the exception to the rule must have occurred and the more developed mind must have happened. No wonder the Romany's could tell fortunes as they were probably tipped off by the Dimension people as we become more intelligent in time when in the Dimension and have so much wisdom to share with us, which up till recently has been a struggle for them to make us understand that they are there.

The travelling in time theory that some books speak of, may I think, have evolved out of the fact that the Dimension people can store memory and calculate how the future can develop. I must be careful when writing about time travel as it is only my personal opinion that they just have twenty-four hours in their day like we do. There are many books on this subject and they may well be accurate. The main thing with this one is for us to understand the effects of the backlog trauma.

The group of Dimension people who are organising this book, may wish to cover other aspects with a sequel, or even leave it to other writers. In time we shall see. In my own case I have only been able to hear single words or phrases but always they are relevant to the code guidance.

I must have the mind of the future for them to guide

me into writing Josh's message about the little dog. It was accompanied by a racing metabolism and although it did no harm they had to think of a way to guide me without the physical discomfort. It is obvious that my mind is not so evolved as DORIS'S, but who's COMPLAINING?

The clues carry on so much that it would take too long to record them all but I am convinced that I have got it right about DORIS and am happy to see that her books are in great demand. Among them are VOICES IN MY EAR, and INNOCENT VOICES IN MY EAR. That one is about children. She says that sometimes at night she has to, sort of 'switch them off' as the are so anxious to make us understand, that they are there, that lots would try to talk at once. What a lot we owe to people like her who OPENED THE DOOR TO THE OTHER DIMENSION. All the evening after The BOOK TOWN, Telly programmes were jogging my memory of her. I should have 'twigged' my father wanted to think of DORIS and MUSIC. In one programme there were about THIRTY FIVE CHILDREN. ALL PLAYING CELLOS!

All those PIANOS! All those STEAM TRAINS! And ALL THOSE GOLDEN WEDDING CLOCKS! We've got to hand it to them THEY'RE TRIERS.

Just as I had written that, ALEX was playing a recording of a melody (Blissfully unaware of what I was writing)

THROUGH MY DOOR OF DREAMS

Shortly after a television programme came up entitled HAVE I BEEN HERE BEFORE? This is a experiment where several celebrities underwent a kind of regression into their past lives. It was astonishing how many facts they were able to find to back up the past life theory.

As the people taking part seemed to relive short periods of time I must keep an open mind.

Their experience could be a form of TIME TRAVEL.

Not far away from the ABBEY TOWN is a huge hill. I found it by accident one day before my trip to Scotland. All around were the most glorious views. No matter how far I looked I could see no sign of pollution or anything that could mar it's beauty. It was that day I knew that we must be eternal and everything that lives now is permanent in some way, but I had no idea how it could be, only absolute certainty that it was so. I parked the bike and happily burst into song.

 THE SOUND OF MUSIC

Half way to the ABBEY one day, stretching across the sky were black clouds, behind them the most spectacular SILVER LINING. I have never seen anything like it except in those old paintings with a religious theme so I stopped the bike to look. Cars came by and to my surprise carried on regardless; puzzling, as the rays were extraordinarily beautiful. I felt shaken as there seemed no logical explanation, I thought, perhaps my theory that all could be explained was incorrect.

As the days went on more information came in - To record it all would take too much space, but the explanation was simple. There were three jumble sales at different times. TWO O'CLOCK, TWO THIRTY and THREE O'CLOCK, a few miles in between each. One in the village to the left of me, one to the right and one at the ABBEY TOWN. On the road that I was on.

I didn't decide which jumble I was going to until ONE O'CLOCK.

The Dimension people can WEATHER FORECAST.

They knew that autumn was going to provide us with some interesting cloud formation and that it was going to stretch across a wide area that day, so they influenced people to organise jumble sales in that direction they were safe with three then waited until ONE 'O'CLOCK, before making me chose the one that was going to be in the most spectacular place. they probably had to wait to see themselves where it was going to turn up the best, so of course the amazing display was just over the road that I had chosen.

Behind there was only blue sky and of course no jumbles in that direction. They went on to explain that the reason why other vehicles didn't stop was because THEY CAN MAKE ME SEE SUN RAYS MORE VIVIDLY THAN OTHERS, and sort of sharpen my perspective.

A couple of days later I met the postman with the returned manuscript feeling sad, went off on the bike as I was riding along, I could see the huge abbey town hill where I had sung THE SOUND OF MUSIC. Right over it was another SILVER LINING, spectacular and beautiful, directly over where I had found such JOY. When I got home, ALEX was playing his music,

 LOOK FOR THE SILVER LINING

It was the ABBEY TOWN where I saw the painting of the STEAM TRAIN and the pictures in the cafe. It strikes me that JIMMY is very fond of the ABBEY TOWN.

I needed stuff for urgently for the shop as I was afraid the teeth and bike would go again. You would think that I would have more faith by now wouldn't you?

On my way to a village jumble sale, It's opening,

TWO THIRTY. I came to a railway bridge. There were lots of people with cameras 'Happy as crickets' who said the FLYING SCOTSMAN was due to leave the ABBEY TOWN at TWO-FIFTEEN. And was reminded of the Welcome back painting at the OLDE TYME FAYRE. I sadly carried on my way, as I was afraid to be late arriving at the hall with ten minutes to spare, so if I had just had trust in the Dimension guidance, I still could have seen the train.

In an advertisement paper it said the FLYING SCOTSMAN was coming again the following week, so I planned a jumble in the ABBEY TOWN. I set off in plenty of time to look for a vantage spot but when I got there I couldn't find the hall where the jumble sale was to be held. Now I go through that town every week, but for the life of me I couldn't find the hall. It was like the day I couldn't remember Sylvia's name. When I did eventually find the hall there was no time left to look for the vantage spot as it was nearly time for the jumble sale.

Standing in the queue at exactly TWO TWENTY-FOUR when I heard the train. It came closer and closer and became so loud, like it was just beyond the hedge I have never been the steam addict my brother is (It is logical that he would be married to the daughter of an engine driver) I can fall in love with anything if I can travel in it) but as she came close she BLEW HER WHISTLE. It was so loud but such a lovely sound I wouldn't have missed it for anything. The people in the queue seemed not to notice so I was puzzled.

When riding through the ABBEY TOWN again I saw that the railway lines were a long way from the hall and although it seemed that they were just over the hedge they were too far away for the sound to be so clear. Even with the wind in the right direction it still would have been impossible in the normal way, for it to sound so loud.

THE Dimension people hadn't, meant me to be at the vantage spot, so I was deliberately made to forget the whereabouts of the hall and the railway lines, so that they could teach us how they can sharpen our senses to sound and sight.

I found everything I needed at the jumble sale. It is time I learned to have confidence in THE PEOPLE IN THE DRIVING SEAT. Of course this is explaining how they are doing it. Our perspective is sharpened so that the one remark in a film or book can be more clear than the rest and like the colours in the kitchen and the field that day. I was reminded of a piece of music that I was struggling to play in the beginning of this experience, from the musical SOUTH PACIFIC. It is called

   YOU'VE GOT TO BE CAREFULLY TAUGHT

This song actually has a negative theme, but the Dimension group has made it clear that the negative must be reversed.

About this time THE SOUND OF MUSIC came up again with the song, as the hills were reflecting in a bus window

   I HAVE CONFIDENCE IN MEE (MEE)

It is definitely time I did.

One day later on in the year I had the unfortunate experience of having TWO fears stopped in one day. (No room here for all the details), I had found a copy of ARTHUR MEES ENGLAND quite valuable series. And as it was near Christmas the proceeds would help towards the expenses that had worried me. I rode home singing happily, completely forgetting about backlog reactions.

I sat down to study the telly programmes to see that THE SOUND OF MUSIC was scheduled for the next day. Suddenly my mind started to fill with odd things, I thought, light headed? So I said to myself, stay calm and the and the Dimension people will tell me what is wrong. Could it be over tiredness? I put some music on and a HUNGARIAN Rhapsody was playing, so I thought DAD please help me. It was more severe than ever before, like the horrid feeling that some people experience when at a great height. I forced down some food as hunger can make us have some odd reactions too.

A knock came at the door, it was a young boy. He wanted to make a Christmas decoration because he didn't have anything to do and "Did I have a LOG? I said "We'll have a look round the BACK to see what we can find and I was so grateful for the diversion he picked up a BRUSH-HEAD before finding the right shaped one, then took TWO LOGS. I came back indoors when he had gone, then it dawned! No wonder!

I'd had TWO worries brought to an end that day, ITS BACKLOG! DOUBLE BACKLOG! And the BRUSH HEAD?

My grandmother who is in the Dimension uses the song from SALAD DAYS.

 GET YOURSELF SOMETHING TO DO DEAR

and the words so comforting from the show

 WILD VIOLETS DON'T SAY GOOD BYE

Well we don't have to say goodbye do we?

So I stopped worrying and prepared to wait until it went away. I got out the hoover and gave the floor a good old clean. By the time it was done the horrid thing was nearly gone. It returned slightly the next morning having recharged the 'battery' the previous day a tiny bit with alarm, but it was soon over. I thought I shall now get organised to watch THE SOUND OF MUSIC and look forward to the lovely rendering of

 I HAVE CONFIDENCE IN ME

From then on the colour VIOLET has always been associated with my grandmother'

BILL POWELL transitioned, can't call it dying any more. ALEX told me at five thirty one Monday evening. I used to know ROSE, BILLS wife years ago and engaged to her brother VICTOR was almost one of her wonderful family. When VICTOR and I broke off our engagement we still stayed in touch for a little while.

In those days though, without transport we couldn't get to see our friends, even when they may be only a few miles away. When I did become mobile, years had passed and I didn't like to just turn up.

On the morning after ALEX told me, I had this longing to be with her but I was in a terrible quandary whether or no to go and pay a visit. One is always afraid of making things worse. I decided to tidy up a box of hair curlers; very out of character as that morning or any morning for that matter, tidying up was not my first consideration. I came across A POWDER COMPACT. Inside it was the brand name which was ROSES full Christian and surname before she was married and when I knew her It repeated underneath and bore in mind that to distinguish things from accidents they have to repeat or link in some way. On the lid was a basket of flowers.

Not long before my mother left us and during the time I was with VIC, who is in the Dimension now, she embroidered a design of basket of flowers and framed it. Not having done any embroidery for years I was surprised when she suddenly did that. It was incomplete too, so I didn't care for it. She wasn't interested enough, having done so much in the past and taken it for granted like SYLVIA did with her dancing Normally she could make flowers live. The little basket of flowers on the compact lid didn't have the overlapping edge either so I decided to chance it and go over to see ROSE.

When she opened the door she was so glad to see me. It was as though it was only yesterday that I had seen her last. On the wall there was a picture of a JOCKEY WITH HIS CAP TURNED BACK! I couldn't keep my eyes off it. After learned that BILL had painted it himself. I told her of my experiences but she was not as surprised as some, as she, as a teenager had known strange things of her own, and I believe ROSE and BILL have more than a bit of mixed background.

A couple of days later in a local news programme was an artist in the act of painting a picture of ... A JOCKEY WITH HIS CAP TURNED BACK.
It was amazing how like the one in BILLS painting it was.

The Sunday after a film came up starring CARY GRANT. BILL was so like him to look at, one expects CARY To sing the SEPTEMBER SONG or say "BY JINGO" as he used to do. I gave ROSE all the notes on the manuscript to read and worried for days in case she should go into the backlog trauma.

The expression 'THINK PINK' kept coming up in magazines and telly and the happy day dawned when I had a letter to say that she loved the notes, and was sorry when they ended.

On my next visit I left her just before a shower of rain. On one side of the road a RAINBOW started to form; in a field opposite the other end had begun too. I stopped, cars going past, and slowly the centre filled in to form a complete bow.

Like my friendship with ROSE, the RAINBOW closed up and became as though it had never been separated. A little Aircraft began circling as though it was going through it, like a tiny silver bird glinting in the sun.

When I got home and picking greens in the garden, another two little planes began circling exactly over my head, in the sunshine SPEEDWELLS were shining up at me. Strains of a song currently playing in the kitchen.....

♪
    BIRDS FLY OVER THE RAINBOW
    WHY THEN OH WHY CAN' I

♪

One day when I was in a hurry I grabbed a jersey that I had bought at a jumble sale the day before. In the mirror I saw reflected a BIG PINK ROSE I caught sight of a gardening paper, on the cover advertised a BLUE ROSE and inside another. The only time I have seen BLUE ROSES was when a friend said "They turn back to PINK in time." I expect Horticulturists have overcome this problem now as that was sometime ago.

Propped up on the piano was the song, RED ROSES FOR A BLUE LADY (Musical notes please)

The PINK ROSE on my jersey was reversed in the MIRROR while ALEX burst into that song with that tune too; I thought "Could ROSE be BLUE? The expression THINK PINK kept coming up on the telly and advertisements, so I wondered, perhaps it was time to visit her. I found ROSE very sad. She missed her dear BILL dreadfully. She said "It looks as if this is only meant for you CON, as I haven't had a `dicky bird' "

Not a sign had she been given, and very disappointed she was too.

We know now that her high misery level would have affected her ability to pick up the code but I was able to cheer her a little, and we ended rolling around with laughter at some of the Dimension antics.

We recalled the day that BILL had driven us to PORTLAND LIGHTHOUSE. And she got out photos. In one BILL is holding a MUG and, in another he is IN THE DRIVING SEAT OF HIS CAR. ROSE had felt the need to snap him as he was driving along.

In my next box of odds, there was a LITTLE BROWN JUG. On it PORTLAND BILL. Little jugs started to do the `breakfast dinner and tea' stunt' that by now I was getting familiar with, nearly always BROWN ones and little ones. And the song goes

♪ HA HA HA YOU AND ME LITTLE BROWN JUG... ♪

One day the auctioneer said....
"WHAT AM I BID FOR A BIG BROWN JUG?"
I thought "That's curious, surely the Dps could count on DICKIE to get things right"
Following this, ROSE, was showing me lovely china that BILL had given her. Among it an old antique JUG.
I turned it upside down to see the makers mark which was BP. BILLS initials, REVERSED. Hence the BIG BROWN JUG. (Opposite way round) And the song goes ....

♪   I DO LOVE THEE   ♪

Shortly after a film, and the last words before the end CARY GRANT says to the girl who is his wife in real life.
"I HAPPEN TO LOVE YOU VERY MUCH MRS ROSE"
The film is full of courage and compassion and is based on a story called ROOM FOR ONE MORE.
I am unable to complete this story, but the film contains much parallel with ROSE and BILLS experience. But one must observe privacy.

The first anniversary of my trip to SCOTLAND came along, Two days before the date of BRIGADOON DAY a film of the place where I had met all the people from different parts of the world and the next day there was a reference to the musical BRIGADOON. I was the day before though, I was wondering why all the linking things were happening before.

In the morning after the films I had to see the Dentist. I had no worries about it, it was simply that my teeth had to be seen to. He couldn't fit me in during the morning; unusual as he is so accommodating in an emergency. I understood and went home to return in the afternoon.

It had been raining. On my way there was a detour, I had to go a long way round to approach the town by a different way. This must have altered my timing a bit it is unusual to go that way and at that time of day.

As I went over a bridge GOSH! I couldn't believe my eyes THERE WAS A RAINBOW ON THE RIVER! AND THAT WAS BRIGADOON DAY.

Every year the anniversary was observed unfailingly. One year when I was listening to a recording of a Christian song, I looked up to see that the picture on the wall of JESUS knocking on the door was bathed in an oblong of GOLDEN LIGHT. The shaft of sunlight through the window exactly framing the window. The Dimension people must have noticed that the patch of light falls on the wall at sunrise in October. The BRIGADOON trip was the second week in that month. ALEX must have been made to hang the picture in the right place. I made a mental note to photograph it when it happened again, but double glazing was put into our home and to my dismay found the light was altered with the new window shape. As time went by a new tree grew in the garden. The sunlight began to shine through its swaying branches causing the GOLDEN LIGHT to flicker on the picture, seeming to give the figure life and movement. The effect was as glorious as the original.

I think the whole colourful plan was thought out around weather conditions, as they must be able to forecast them roughly months ahead, I found in a box of `odds a dictionary of films. All had been watched by a team of people who made criticisms of the standard. Our DP group must influence the programme editors which, to chose, or what could be even more likely, they; influenced the films when they were being made, then organised events to coincide with them.

For example, an, advertisement for ALL BRAN, where a little boy says "CONCENTRATED WHAT'S CONCENTRATED?" At the same time they see that I am eating ALL BRAN "CONCENTRATE CON."

Then that will be followed by a film or play and the people in the film or play will be wearing a HAT similar to the one I've seen in the jumble sale that day and then another film will come up soon after, REPEATING THE HAT. Another example, I got a 1930s CLOCK, and that same afternoon saw one exactly like it in a film. This became more frequent, now they do them every day. Of course, they probably had been doing so all along, but it took two years for me to get even remotely proficient in deciphering the code.

As time went on, there were more stories concerning BILL and ROSE. BILL uses racing and many have sequels, there's no room to include them here.

Whenever it was time to go over and see ROSE, as well as PINK things and ROSES, they use those ARUM

LOLLIES. So, I duly did what I was asked and just after the BRIGADOON ANNIVERSARY, and went over to see her. I told her about the `RAINBOW' ON THE RIVER' and she produced a painting by BILL of the SAME BRIDGE.

About this time I found in another box, MUSIC, together with a song book. In it the titles; LAVENDER BLUE, and FOREVER AND EVER.

Once I sang the first to VICTOR and he sang FOREVER AND EVER to my strumming on an old piano.

When on a shopping trip, I ran into an old friend who used to live in a little tucked away village where I had worked in the big house as a maid. VIC and ROSE lived there too. URSULA had to go to work, so after a hurried word we said goodbye.

Months later I took another trip there quietly singing to myself

♪ LAVENDER BLUE DILLY DILLY LAVENDER GREEN
♪

There she was walking towards me. This time I was invited to her home for coffee. I was amazed at how much we had in common and surprised that I hadn't I hadn't got to know her more when we lived in the tucked away village. VIC used to talk of her and say "She makes me laugh" meaning that she was such fun to be with, his affection brotherly ... She never met anyone that she liked enough to marry. When it was time to leave, she gave me some flowers.

I still had a little vase on the kitchen window sill. All through the summer it was never empty; as soon as the flowers faded someone gave me more.

One morning I was wondering what would happen in the winter and would they stop coming? When I noticed the flowers that my friend had given me were like SEA LAVENDER. (It grows on the NORFOLK COAST where I lived, long ago and far away as a child). They dry and become EVERLASTING. (Static) I went out straight away in a different direction than usual, parked the bike, unaware until I returned, that it was directly opposite a shop door, over it, the name DILLYS.

The next morning I settled down to write to ROSE and tell her of the LAVENDER BLUE. When I overheard ALEX say as he was showing his brother photos.

"THAT'S VIC WITH SING"

"WHOSE SING?"

ALEX replied "VIC'S DAD IS NAMED `SING' "

VIC was stationed in SINGAPORE when in the army. And his dad used to talk about SINGAPORE and FAR AWAY PLACES, and SING was a nickname. Immediately afterwards the telly went on about a tourist place that I had visited with him the only time I ever went there. The same place came up again a few days later for the second time. On the piano was a copy of the song FAR AWAY PLACES

On the same evening of the photographs, ALEX called "COME IN HERE AND LISTEN TO THIS" The radio was playing Vic's song and in my mind I could hear his BING like rendering of,

FAR AWAY PLACES

I leave it to you to guess what he was telling us. The

document goes, ONE SPECIAL PERSON WHO WE WAIT FOR .... And real love like the LAVENDER BLUE flowers lasts FOREVER AND EVER ....

URSULA'S name came up repeatedly afterwards, sure enough after I had finished writing this someone called her name in a film. They must be working out how long it is going to take me to write the stories so it looks as if I must be up to schedule.

I had been worrying that I was slow in getting the book done, so anticipated staying up half the night although dreadfully tired, but have had my attention drawn to a film that CARY GRANT made, as well as SINGAPORE LADY, (The name of a plane,) I had wondered where it came in though, as it seemed to have no significance but I've got it now. It is entitled WALK DON'T RUN.

After the LAVENDER BLUE Story LAVENDER BAGS kept turning up I'm snowed up with them now, We'll have to have an extension put on the house at the rate they are coming in.

After I had written that, a little girl came up to me at a jumble sale and said "HERE'S A LAVENDER BAG FOR YOU"

Early IN THE 1950s THE MOON WENT BLUE! VIC used to meet me in the evening from work at the big house. One night he exclaimed "LOOK THE MOON IS BLUE!"

It came up on the radio the next day with the explanation that it was caused by dust from Canadian forest fires.

VIC uses the song BLUE MOON and look! .... A BLUE ROSE

BLUE MOON

A gardening advertisement and the following telly ad:
along with others

(Film the Moon is Blue (!1976 U)

Innuendo laden comedy romance with William
Holden** 96587865

See what I mean about not overcrowding the book? As they
keep it up continually?

At the market I bought FAGGOTS, These are a
traditional dish popular in the south of England and are
delicious. They were a bit too salty so I told the stall owner
who was grateful that I had pointed it out to him, these
being his first of a new venture.

When I got home I noticed the kitchen was full of salt
pots, pepper pots too. All over the place. Umpteen out of
one box and others that had been accumulating for weeks.
That same evening ALEX came home with FAGGOTS. I
should have suspected but didn't especially when I had
bought a big white pot, on it the word in huge letters SALT.
As I was examining it for the shop found the underneath
rim was chipped, although perfectly usable not suitable for
resale. And surely I had seen it somewhere before? IT WAS
MY OWN! I had given it to a friend and she had passed it
on to the Scouts jumble sale. I found too I had bought my

own sugar bowl as well.

The evening after the FAGGOTS a knock came at the door and there was an old friend I hadn't seen for years. Have only met BOB once since I used to stay with his mum ANNE before I was married. His face so strained and white, he had so kindly come thirty eight miles on a motor bike to tell us that his step dad had transitioned into the Dimension. PAUL used to live along side of us in the tucked away village. When they married he and ANNE had a little house right beside the railway lines. When the trains went by the salt and pepper pots used to vibrate.

A particularly noisy train made them SHAKE and RATTLE and she used to make FAGGOTS and sell them.

ANNE was already in the Dimension and up till then her identity hadn't come in. I was in a quandary whether or not to tell BOB about the coincidences. The trouble is that when we have just lost someone, our misery generator is going round at a faster than ever before. Immediately after a bereavement is not the best time to have our fears stopped.

As he and ALEX were talking, in my mind I asked the Dimension people what to do when suddenly I remembered ANNE had a foreign sounding name. Although she was English her attractive continental beauty may come from other shores YES! so I decided to tell him. He said "WE HAD FAGGOTS FOR TEA YESTERDAY FOR THE FIRST TIME IN TWO YEARS."

I have never seen a face come back to life so fast. I put my arms around him and we were half laughing and half crying, mind you, the laughter won. I gave him the current record that had been playing that day. ANNE spoke with a low contralto voice. The song on the record was sung by an artist with the rich contralto tones she used to use and the

words go so lovingly

 FOLD YOUR WINGS OF LOVE AROUND ME

Anne loved the IVOR NOVELLO songs.

I still worried in case he went into the backlog trauma as its onset can be delayed for quite a while sometimes, although reassurance came time and time again on the dimension code. Then one day ALEX said "THERE'S A MESSAGE FROM BOB ON THE CB, HE SENDS HIS LOVE."

Next day I bid what I thought was a box of china. When close found that I was the proud owner of THIRTY SEVEN SALT AND PEPPER POTS!

Now if you think that this couldn't happen to you, A Little warning. A couple of weeks back, within a short time of each other, different people wanted to give us FIVE SOFAS!

Shortly after ANNA came in said …

"I'm GETTING A NEW SOFA CON, WONDERED IF YOU WOULD LIKE THE OLD ONE, AS IT'S STILL QUITE GOOD"

There was such a puzzled expression on her face when we burst into laughter"

One cold and rainy day a market holder decided to pack up. He started to sing

 TIME TO GO HOME, TIME TO GO HOME

The song is from a television series for children that was very popular before the programme became so sophisticated called ANDY PANDY. I am happy to see that this charming series has been revived after many years with other delightful characters from "WATCH WITH MOTHER"

 TIME TO GO HOME, TIME TO GO HOME

The song is from a television series for children that was very popular before the programme became so sophisticated called ANDY PANDY. I am happy to see that this charming series has been revived after many years with other delightful characters from "WATCH WITH MOTHER before programmes became so sophisticated called ANDY PANDY. I am happy to see that this charming series has been revived after so many years with other delightful characters from 'WATCH WITH MOTHER`

The next day I set off to catch a bus to a completely new town, but before leaving, I noticed a new clock that Alex had hung on the wall with a PENDULUM. On the way, there was a street with my mother's name and simultaneously a lady on the bus asked me the time, afterwards, realised my attention was being sought. On arrival I spotted a little child wearing an ANDY PANDY pyjama suit in his push chair and going into a store. Remembering the song, I followed and what should I see there but rows and rows of CLOCKS.

The first dozen had pendulums and the rest (There were eighty before losing count) were round, some with happy faces like the one I had painted for the kitchen scene in our production of CINDERELLA. The lot were all working at once, the entire wall covered with them Up till then a dozen identities had come in. They were easy enough to recognise. Similar dodges like the steam trains and the embroidered picture applied to them all one by one. The clocks were a tip off that there were more people in our Dimension group than I had realised.

A lovely friend who lives a few doors away invited me in for a chat one afternoon. I thought how cosy her room was and I enjoyed the comfort of her armchair and delightful company. As three o' clock chimed, I didn't take much notice until a little while after another one chimed. I began to register when still ANOTHER joined in `CUCKOO CUCKOO'

This was merrily accompanied by `CHEEP CHEEP' from a watch lying on a side table. I said "Goodness, how many clocks have you got?" And would you believe it? There was one exactly like the GOLDEN WEDDING CLOCK! Isn't it priceless? She has a beloved cat. At night she calls him home so that he can be safe and warm. His name is ANDY PANDY, (PANDY for short).

I think they are saying that in TIME we will find answers to our problems as there are now so many of them to guide us and that it is only a matter of TIME before we can all 'COME IN OUT OF THE COLD' so to speak. That may explain why they keep on about FURRY COATS too. I think they are saying that they've got us 'ALL WRAPPED UP'.

As I write I hear the strains of a song coming from the telly accompanying an advertisement for sofas...

 IT'S A WONDERFUL WORLD

OH! THE SOFAS! At the beginning of the ANDY PANDY films a posh little voice says ....

"ARE YOU SITTING COMFORTABLY?

They don't leave it there; as soon as I wrote this, up it comes again! Would you believe it?

Are you sitting comfortably sir?

Are you sitting comfortably ...?

Are you sitting comfortably sir?

Are you sitting comfortably ...?

Are you really sitting comfortably?

Are you <u>really</u> sitting comfortably?
As I write ALEX is playing his music again; THERE'S

NO PLACE LIKE HOME As I WAS checking this page ALEX received a birthday card from LINDA. It had six children in a row looking over a fence into a field. They are avidly watched by a dog just like our dear old DANNY. (BELLES STORY). BELLE was DANNY'S previous owner.

The brand name of the card was ROYLE. The DP's have been on about ROYALTY for some time. Now what are they saying I wonder?

It was about fifteen months since the rainbow in the field and THE LITTLE DOG story. The next day the identities really got going. Over a period of time they came in two by two and to my astonishment they were everyone I had known except for a few. It was explained why they wouldn't be mentioned until later. I was a bit worried about AUNT DAISY (Tony's mum). She didn't turn up with the others, then one day I noticed double daisies in JOSH'S garden, and sure enough even though it wasn't yet spring, all the field was covered with them. Hundreds, the Dimension people must have had to wait until they came out before her identity could come in. Soon came the song IN THE GOOD OLD SUMMER TIME. There was good reason for why they wanted to make the most of AUNT DAISY as they later proved.

While watching a film and catching bits of the dialogue that were relevant, I noticed too that the opening number was the same song that I had sung during our last production in which we used a NAUTICAL theme. Halfway through the dialogue goes...

"I'LL PAY FOR THE DISHES."

By a waitress, having dropped a tray full.

The day before I had seen a broken vegetable dish identical to the china that I had dropped, whilst working in the big house as a maid in the tucked away village. I used to break things all the time. Of course, once I had begun to worry, the worse it became and was in danger of going through the whole lot, always saying ...

"I'LL PAY FOR THE DISHES."

I never had to pay for them; the lady in the big house was so understanding about it and knew that there was some reason for the unfortunate tendency. My time with her was of the highest importance.

We had a gardener who was retired from the ROYAL NAVY. One day he left the radio on using up the battery). The lady thought I had done it. She believed me when I said I hadn't, but it remained a mystery to her as I couldn't very well `split' on NOBBY, PETTY OFFICER CLARKE, (actually CHIEF PETTY OFFICER I mean, sorry NOBBY). By using the dialogue and linking it with events at the auction, he was able to say, "SORRY ABOUT THE RADIO." After the dialogue film, all the sailors came in UNCLE GEORGE, ex-NAVAL MARINE used without a shadow of a doubt THE DRINKING SONG and OLD FATHER THAMES another one he used to sing. COMMANDER BOYD too. Together we had taken part in a play, I IMS PINAFORE, where he had to use his own uniform. I le had trouble with the sword as it swung around a bit when we danced.

At the auction a NAVAL SWORD for sale NAVAL OFFICER'S DRESS UNIFORM too. Couldn't miss him, well couldn't miss any of them really, especially when a film came on of a young man in a NAVAL OFFICER'S uniform, several times falling head first, having merrily tripped over his sword (CARRY ON ADMIRAL).

It was COMMANDER BOYD who revived my interest in Christianity, which was to play a vital role in the plans to get our attention. The Christian teaching of the POWER OF COMPASSION was essential and without it none of this would, in my own case, have come about I am sure. I do not mean that other religions are not powerful in teaching love and joy — of course they are. Collectively they must have been responsible for saving the whole lot.

Although COMMANDER BOYD was terminally ill, he coped with it so serenely that no one could know him without realising that something spectacular was keeping him going, just as NAT handles his problems so amazingly with his trust in JESUS.

Mind you, JESUS is a superstar, no wonder he is called 'THE SON OF GOD'.

As I write this the strains of a dramatic melody are coming from the living room ...

  JESUS CHRIST SUPERSTAR

When the identities came in they were too many to record. The lovely BUTCHER and BAKER who used to call at the big house both turned up. I kept seeing BATHTUBS everywhere. In a field, gardens and yards. Also, a turquoise green one; that Verdigris colour that copper goes when it is old, and a play — THREE MEN IN A BOAT. One day SYLVIA was out with her dogs when she found some BATH TAPS; exactly what she needed too. On the news a story of some people who were shipwrecked. The only things they had to cling to were two BATH TUBS! Wished I had taken more notice of that story - it was quite a while before I saw the connection.

I was rubbing myself down after a bath two days

later when it dawned on me. The old rhyme goes ...

RUB A DUB DUB, THREE. MEN IN A TUB, THE
BUTCHER, THE BAKER, THE CANDLESTICK MAKER,
ALL POPPED OUT OF A HOT POTATO.

Thinking as I was dressing, or was it a cold potato?
When a huge hole appeared in my tights and my heel
POPPED OUT like a BIG POTATO!

But where was THE CANDLESTICK MAKER?

Shortly after a new identity came in. Once, for a
concert, I was asked to sing the song

  OTHER PEOPLE'S BABIES

This is a song of a children's nanny.

As a young girl of fifteen I had taken a job as a
nursemaid. This was when we were in the north country.
The lady who I worked for and her family were so loving
and kind. They had a beautiful old house and I was so
happy with them. We had to come south; it was my fault
that I didn't keep in touch. The last time I saw her she was
wearing a big wide-brimmed hat and looked like MRS
MINIVER in the famous film. I have never forgotten her; so
good so fair. She gave me a little book of Dickens, A
CHRISTMAS CAROL and still have it.

The day after I had written THE THREE MEN IN A
TUB story, the little book turned up at the jumble sale.
Exactly the same version. I bought it and thought of her
straight away. The clues came in again and again. She must
have remembered everything we had done after all this
time. It would be fun to record it all but it would take too
much space. There can be no mistake as the law of averages

couldn't produce so many linking things. In several films' ladies wearing big hats and her name was in so many of the clues.

It was just after the war; we couldn't get any work done in those days as so many skilled people were in the forces. They had some copper pipes that used to make the washing green, turquoise green. Of course, they would have got them fixed when workmen became available. Then those things were unavoidable. She used the COPPER pipes in her identity clues (and I've just remembered that I sang RUB A DUB DUB to her little girl). How comforting it is to think of her in my life again after so long and now I have TWO copies of A CHRISTMAS CAROL.

When I had written this story, I searched for the original book, but was confronted with boxes and boxes of articles. My cupboards are full up as I have been trying to keep all the things they are using for the code and I didn't have time to find it. A couple of days later, auction Monday, I found another identical copy and have never seen one like it since.

More identities of other employers came up. As I didn't stay anywhere long, I had got to know a lot of people. The babies theme kept up, like references to JELLY MOULDS. At the dinner table once I went to turn out a blancmange from one. It was perfect, couldn't have wished for a better shape except that it landed beautifully on the tablecloth. Once a little one went missing. Sure enough two programmes on kids who went missing, all were quite safe though thank goodness. Oh dear, they don't forget, do they? I didn't rate too high in the nanny stakes I'm afraid.

I have around a string of pretty blue beads. Every time they've caught my eye, I have remembered a film,

RANDOM HARVEST, acted by the same artist as MRS MINIVER with RONALD COLMAN. He plays a First World War soldier who suffered from shell shock. The same thing happened to my father so I should have known that they would use it somehow[7].

After a time of perfect happiness, he goes out one day and just as my father did, loses his memory. The three years of happiness a blank, she finds him and one day to make him remember says poignantly, holding a string of BLUE BEADS up to her face ...

"HE SAID THEY WERE THE COLOUR OF MY EYES ..."

That week of the blue beads I found the book of the film.

Thinking about my former employer and how kind and understanding she was and wondering if she had been in the original plans as others have, instantly A CHRISTMAS CAROL caught my eye. It was UPSIDE DOWN, I don't think she was in the original plans as others have been but instead, a wonderful, loving, useful RANDOM HARVEST.

Soon after getting the idea a song came along, HOORAY FOR HOLLYWOOD.

You're telling me ...

I had to keep leaving this to turn off a dripping tap. It was the BATH and OH DEAR! It is turning GREEN! Hadn't noticed that before, we must have copper pipes then.

NAT collects stage biographies. One day he went to mention an old music hall artist he was reading up on when he suddenly couldn't remember his name. (There we go again). Then he caught sight of an old antique postcard photo I had put on the piano after finding it in a box of `odds and ends' and exclaimed ...

"THERE IT IS THAT'S HIM, GEORGE ARLISS."

I said, "DO YOU OFTEN HAVE COINCIDENCE NAT?"

He replied, "ALL THE TIME. IT'S A WAY OF LIFE."

The night before auction day I was playing a recording of OLD MUSIC HALL SONGS. In the middle the music breaks off giving way to OI1 FOR THE WINGS OF A DOVE.

The next day at the auction, along came the lorry with our little brother's name on the side. (The auction being in the open air). I pulled up in the car park to see that the next car to me had a slogan written in the back window, `THANK GOD FOR JESUS'. Sure enough there he was.

NAT has taken up embroidery as his many interests do have to be easy on his physical strength and I was ASTONISHED. "On his jacket were a KINGFISHER, DAISIES, JESUS along with a DOVE OF PEACE. Things that have been mentioned in these records, nearly all in the same stitch as my mother's picture. HONEYSUCKLE that my father had reminded me of in one of his stories. (All too many to include) was growing out of his pocket. I said, "HONEYSUCKLE NAT?" and he replied, "YES, THAT'S

WHERE I KEEP THE FERTILISER ..."

There was a religious badge, on it a CANDLE STICK! That's it! NAT is the CANDLE STICK MAKER.

I was moved and could suddenly see why people do need a little time to GET USED TO THE LIGHT.'

He had been made to park his car so that it was facing a different direction than usual. As he was sitting in the driving seat the SUN RAYS came again in the sky, like on the day of the silver lining, they were exactly in front of him. I said, "CAN YOU SEE THE SUN RAYS NAT?" he answered, "OF COURSE."

"OH, THANK GOD FOR JESUS."

As I write music is playing, an old number ...

IT'S RAINING SUNBEAMS a song that refers to a WEATHER BUREAU.

ALEX has just come in, and tapped his BAROMETER.

There is a lovely story of ALEX, PEGASUS and a BAROMETER but no room to include it here. Perhaps a sequel can be written one day. We shall have to see what transpires.

After I had written this, I had second thoughts about whether I had made the right decision to exclude it, so I have left it to the editors to decide if there is room for just one more story.

I bid for a BAROMETER. Got it for FIFTY PENCE. The arrow was set at CHANGE. ALEX was delighted with it.

He is so stalwart and kind, and has hardly missed a day's work in all the time I have known him, as long as he can have a regular routine, he is happy, no amount of bad weather will worry him though he didn't like change. As long as he can have a regular lifestyle, he is happy, but he was an inveterate `stay at home'.

As a young boy, he lived in the tucked away village, a typically countryside life working on a farm and cycling into the little town for recreation.

At nineteen years old he was called up and quickly sent into the AIR BOURNE service where he was found to be adept at radio. I think the multi-heritage showing up even then, but that was his first experience of change. A D-DAY GLIDER and the capture of the PEGASUS BRIDGE, then known as the ORNE BRIDGE, was not exactly the most comfortable way to see the world for the first time.

After his de-mob, he came home from a trip to the seaside only to find his father had joined the Dimension people. It's not surprising that for him travel was always associated with depression.

Last year he read the BRIGADOON STORY and does know now that his poor fellow soldiers who didn't come back weren't left in the cold ground after all.

One day I brought a book of photographs of LONDON TREASURES. Soon after he announced that he was going off to LONDON with a friend. He came home with the most marvellous photos, He is a fabulous photographer, although he has had no training like lots of multi-heritage people, has multi-cap abilities.

The pictures of LONDON TREASURES and THE HOUSEHOLD CAVALRY made a very interesting collection along with a FLYING DISPLAY he got to as well. He had a terrific time. His fear of change completely gone.

One morning on his CB radio, (his codename PEGASUS), "HELLO RED LEADER, COME IN, RED LEADER."

120

"HELLO RED LEADER, HELLO RED LEADER," and a reference to ADAM twice that afternoon a television play and the dialogue went: "HELLO RED LEADER, HELLO RED LEADER."

"PEGASUS HAS TAKEN OFF."

At first ALEX's take-off was a very gentle process so it is appropriate that the aircraft in the play were micro light planes. He has since travelled the length and breadth of ENGLAND and WALES and we have many lovely photographs to remind us.

CLIFF and ADAM are suspect with the influence of this story, but to *try* to write it all would overcrowd the stories.

The following entry to this journal was made later.

On the day of the sunbeams NAT was swinging an elegant CANE, like the ones that Victorian gentlemen used to carry.

At the time he was taking singing lessons and his fine voice in the style of HOWARD KEEL went well with his black hair, dazzling smile, and FANCY TOPPED CANE.

Sometime later, NAT joined the people in the Dimension, so of course like all of them, his identity came in as can be expected in several ways. One took the form of SHOW BOAT the musical. In it the dazzling smile and fine voice of HOWARD KEEL and the FANCY TOPPED CANE, and would you believe it? THE FULL NAME OF OUR LITTLE BROTHER IS IN THE CAPTIONS ...

Once when riding along I noticed nearly every) car that passed me was BLUE. The next day the same thing happened. BLUE as you will remember is associated with ADELE (BLUE DOLLY story). In the original notes I had said that "I wonder if her mother would be finding all her groceries had blue wrappings or something of that sort." When I got home after seeing the BLUR cars, every label, egg box, and wrapping on my shopping, was BLUE!

One day I had to take the bike to be repaired. All the cars parked outside the garage were BLUE, with the ones that passed by they altogether made a dozen. It probably takes a dozen Dimension people to organise a dodge like that. Until then I hadn't realised how organised they have to be. Of course, to get all those cars on the road at the same time would mean a lot of research as the driver's welfare has to be studied carefully.

At the beginning of this experience when my darling friends were in the backlog stage, I got silly about hanging the washing on the line. The fear that someone would be passing by and say something hurtful was only in my own mind but for ages I took it to the launderette.

At the garage the box fell off the bike; all my clothes were scattered. A little boy helped scoop them up so I asked him to HOLD ON to it, while I strapped it on again.

In the workshop sitting on a shelf was a BLUE DOLLY, its caption HEAVEN SENT. A young lady arrived wearing a BLUE JACKET. The name of her motor scooter COMFORT. I went for a walk while the bike was being seen to, relieved that DAVID didn't have to remove the box; and wandered into a churchyard. A little space had been kept for children's graves, one had fresh flowers and was dated thirty-five years ago.

That evening ALEX came in with a free bottle of COMFORT washing conditioner someone had given him.

One morning I arrived at the auction town a bit earlier than usual, all the same quite a few people were about. They seemed to be sort of dodging each other and nearly bumping into me and just missing each other round corners and saying `sorry'. It had happened several times before so it dawned on me that it was too frequent to be accident.

There were children all around too as it was half term. In a shop a little boy ran into me with a <u>bump</u>. He wasn't hurt but the pattern was by then obvious, but why? I wondered.

ALEX had asked me to get some CARROT SEEDS from the gardening centre and said "LOOK OUT FOR THOSE GIANT ONES THAT COME FROM HOLLAND." A lorry parked just outside my window with the name just framed `WINDMILL CAKES'. They do that a lot with commercial vehicles as they have to turn just outside our house. I had no idea what the WINDMILL CAKES were meaning though.

We saw a little boy so fair. I said, "ALL HE NEEDS IS A PAIR OF CLOGS THEN HE'D LOOK A PROPER LITTLE DUTCH BOY."

Someone remarked about how flowers were brought daily from HOLLAND to sell here, reminding me of a show we did with a WINDMILL scene and a crowd of kids in Dutch costume. The song TULIPS FROM AMSTERDAM.

They started on about a story of a little boy in history[7] who was said to have put a finger into the hole in a dyke that was holding the flood waters at bay.

ALEX went on quite a bit about his DUTCH SEED. Vegetables began to be prevalent, people talking about them in overheard conversation, all puzzling though.

The next morning after the bumping incident with the little boy, ALEX was looking out of the bedroom window when he said laughingly, "LOOK, THERE'S TWO COPPERS UP THE ROAD AND ONES TURNED ROUND SUDDENLY AND THEY'VE BUMPED INTO EACH OTHER." We were `tickled pink'. I had said nothing to ALEX about the bumping the day before.

In a jumble sale queue on the day of the bumping I had been fascinated by TWO little babies in their prams both dozing in exactly the same way. There were children catching my eye everywhere.

Of course! Then it dawned, THEY'VE GOT CHILDREN TOO HAVEN'T THEY? And the message?

HOLD ON, HEAVEN SENT COMFORT IS COMING to all, like the people who own the FLOWER, FRUIT AND VEGETABLE SHOP whose baby girl went into the Dimension.

I know it is poignant. If we could try not to cry. They've had so much of it haven't they? Come to think of it though, they are only happy tears after all.

As the weeks went on children's identities came in steadily. In ALEX's gardening paper was a story of a little boy who won the giant vegetable competition who has the same name as one of the Dimension kids. They stuck to the vegetable theme and I got to know when they were around, as people would just be missing me in the street and talking about their CARROTS.

One day I saw little tiny bags of CARROTS in a supermarket. TWO tiny children with their mummy were choosing CARROTS. I said, "CARROTS DARLINGS?"

And they replied, "FOR A DONKEY."

With the gardening paper they were informing us that the kids have joined in the battle to make us know that they are there and it became more obvious as the weeks went by that they were `HAVING A BALL'.

ALEX has just come in with a bag of spring flower bulbs; they are miniature ones and they've started to shoot. Now what do they mean by that I wonder.

On telly one afternoon a famous pianist was saying that his gift was not of his own making but that it came from `somewhere'. The beautiful designs that are appearing in the shops now suggest to me that the clever talented people in the Dimension can somehow inspire our minds to create lovelier things than ever before. In a shop were some tiny models of FAIRY TALE CASTLES, like the ones that I have painted for our show scenery. I always put one in even show like a trade mark. They are becoming numerous like the GOLDEN WEDDING CLOCKS. The possibility is high that they are the product of the coordination that is growing with the multi-heritage becoming more common. Every single person has some natural ability in some direction and the Dimension people can help us make the most of our capability, and direct us into finding out what that is. But they have emphasised that they can't give us help to develop a skill if we haven't got a tendency in the first place. They know better than we do what our natural gifts are.

They say that we often don't realise our own potential and so before long many of us will be quite surprised to discover new directions that we haven't noticed before. How else could the curtain have gone up on our shows?

As a child I had no intention of studying in any way, with the call of the lanes and woods there was no question of practising the piano more than was absolutely necessary. I low could such stuff compare with a cycle ride uphill and down dale, always somewhere new to discover. Even now it is bliss to walk through wind and rain which does puzzle me a bit as rough weather must surely have been a nuisance to my gypsy forebears. But I was perfectly confident that I would one day, and simply took it for granted, be part of this entertainment that is so important to the world. How the dickens I was going to do that I had no idea, but the story of how the dreams or a little harum scarum `LONG AGO AND FAR AWAY, came true, will have to wait until another time. Mind you. The Dimension kids have made no secret of what they think of my piano playing!

All those things like the LANTERN-LIKE ORCHID HOLDER and MOTHERS DAY CARD, why that could have been designed by my mother, HEAVENS! I bet it was and FRED ASTAIRE, is probably at this very moment telling someone;

 LET FACE THE MUSIC AND DANCE

Twenty-four hours after I had written that, `be blowed' if FOLLOW THE FLEET didn't come up on the telly, the film in which FRED sings and dances to that song. In it a girl named CONNIE who owns a SAILING SHIP.

The afternoon of the film I had brought home a smart DRESS SHIRT all pristine in its wrappings; FRED is wearing one in the LET'S FACE THE MUSIC dance.

A couple of days later I came across a video of the film in a charity shop. And not long after this they got into KNIGHTS! KING ARTHUR'S KNIGHTS and his round table, MEDIEVAL KNIGHTS of the time of RICHARD THE LIONHEART, THE ROBIN HOOD ERA and up-to-date MODERN NEW YEAR'S HONOURS KNIGHTS. Why, they even got FRED into a SUIT OF ARMOUR!

Shortly after, they got into the story of CINDERELLA and how her FAIRY GOD MOTHER tells us that, sooner or later OUR CASTLES WILL RISE, meaning that for all of us ... happiness will come.

And the document says ...

... THE VISION OF MUSICIANS AND WRITERS OF FAIRY TALES AND SONGS AND DANCES WITH WHICH HE CHOSE TO WORK ...

I'm beginning to see what it means ...

Out with her dogs one day, SYLVIA found an old coin. After cleaning it she found it to be an old SIXPENCE.

When we were off jumbling, I asked her for something to eat. I hadn't been able to go home for a meal so she gave me some RYE CRISP BREAD (slimming stuff). Don't miss a trick, do they? She said it was sesame seed and called my attention to the fact that this is BIRD SEED. I shoved it in my POCKET. On returning home noted on the side a book "A SONG OF SIXPENCE."

The following Monday out on the road I noticed dead birds. They had been showing up regularly, big black ones. After some time, it struck me that they were always in the same area. It was sometime before I realised this though. In my box of odds that day were TWO of those things that we put in the centre of a PIE to keep the pastry up and later TWO white aprons like the ones I used to wear in the big house when I was a MAID. In another box was a pack of OLD MAID CARDS. (What cheek! Less of the old if you don't mind). The theme persisted as these things do. JILL

128

kept on about how people should take care with pesticides, and being sure to read the directions on the tin properly. The BLACK BIRDS became too frequent to be accidental and I began to gather that there was more behind it. I must say I was still very slow in getting what they were on about Then, quite suddenly it dawned; "TELL THE RSPCA MAN (I see him regularly) ABOUT THE BLACK BIRDS; SOMEONE HAS NOT READ THE LABEL ON THEIR PESTICIDE TIN."

Unfortunately, by the time I had got the hang of the message it was too late to send one to the RSPCA for examination. Never mind, that was a long time ago. I've improved since then. The old rhyme goes ... SING A SONG OF SIX PENCE, A POCKET FULL OF RYE FOUR AND TWENTY BLACK BIRDS BAKED IN A PIE WHEN THE PIE WAS OPENED, THE BIRDS BEGAN TO SING WASN'T THAT A DAINTY DISH TO SET BEFORE THE KING. THE KING WAS IN HIS COUNTING HOUSE COUNTING OUT HIS MONEY THE QUEEN WAS IN THE PARLOUR, EATING BREAD AND HONEY TI I.E. MAID WAS IN THE GARDEN, HANGING OUT THE CLOTHES ALONG CAME A BLACKBIRD AND PECKED OFF HER NOSE.

Even though I was sure that my friends were over their backlog reactions I was still nervous about going into the garden in case someone came along who hadn't recovered.

The SIXPENCE STORY turned up at the same time as the BROKEN DISHES, but I didn't have to pay for the dishes and I didn't have to hang out the clothes either. The lady in the BIG HOUSE used to wash her ow^{7}n smalls and use the laundry so they wanted me to REVERSE something.

"THERE'S NO NEED TO BE AFRAID OF HANGING

OUT THE CLOTHES. NO ONE'S GOING TO PECK YOUR NOSE OFF."

I decided to trust the Dimension people and the first-time hanging stuff on the washing line, a lovely neighbour passed by who had read the BRIGADOON STORY. She stopped to have a happy chat. All was as it had been before. Her backlog which had been quite severe, was over.

ALEX saves up all his little coins in a bottle and was made to count them all in the front room so with a reference to THE KINGS NEW SUIT that took care of the king JILL was telling us how nourishing HONEY was and full of vitamins so that saw to the honey but the QUEEN was missing.

Later ALEX came in holding up a record sleeve. On it a beautiful FAIRY TALE CASTLE. I said, "It's lovely dear but we've already got a copy of THE THREE ELIZABETHS."

This is a piece of music representing three English Queens ELIZABETH the FIRST (*Good* Queen Bess) THE QUEEN MOTHER and our present QUEEN ELIZABETH the SECOND. It was some time before I realised that THE KINGS NEW SUIT does refer to the QUEEN. Like a game of TIDDLY WINKS, they keep on trying.

I was made to see FIVE MAIL VANS all in a row. On their sides a ROYAL CROWN and noticed that the typewriter in my use, is called ROYAL and the other spare one IMPERIAL. I had sent the manuscript sample to BLOOMSBURY in LONDON by post and wondered DOES THE QUEEN HAVE SOMETHING TO DO WITH THE MANUSCRIPT?

The same theme kept turning up; a story of THE QUEEN MOTHER when she went back to a place in

LONDON that had been bombed during the war. She actually remembered a CAT that she had seen, having gone there after the air raids over forty-five years before.

Currently playing is the music from MERRY ENGLAND

In it a reference to the nursery rhyme ... PUSSY CAT PUSSY CAT WHERE HAVE YOU BEEN, I'VE BEEN TO LONDON TO SEE THE QUEEN.

I thought, associations with the QUEEN must have something to do with the manuscript? It came back with the words, THIS IS NOT OUR FIELD.

I expect you're getting this now. The QUEEN went to the cat, not the CAT to the QUEEN (bless her heart) so we have to REVERSE something. Mind you, I did have trouble with my reverses in the beginning but we'll all improve with practise. Of course, I sent the manuscript off again.

The whole meaning of this story was obscure. The possibility is high that I missed some of the clues so have found that when I do, they will often come back with the story and start all over again. We are indeed a game of TIDDLY WINKS.

One market day I was looking for something for a birthday present when I spotted a MUSIC BOX. The man on the stall wound it up to demonstrate that It played the theme from LOVE STORY. It was like a tiny CHEST OF DRAWERS. I kept an open mind and went off to a cafe. Been in there umpteen times but had never noticed before that the proprietor's name was the same as the MUSIC BOX young man in the Dimension.

One day soon after, there was a FIRE SCREEN for sale. It had a CRINOLINE LADY embroidered on it but was grubby. Just as I decided that its condition wasn't good enough, I heard a young girl say "I'M GOING TO BID FOR THAT BOX OF CLOTHES, IT'S GOT SOME OLD DRAWERS, YOU KNOW, THE ONES WITH THE LONG LEGS." I didn't bid for the fire screen. It went for ONE POUND and immediately realised that it was a BLOOMER, as I could have washed it.

It was days before I remembered THE CRINOLINE LADY was wearing DRAWERS with the long legs. They wanted me to get the words BLOOMERS and DRAWERS when later at the jumble sale someone held up a pair of OLD-FASHIONED DRAWERS laughing. Then I began to notice that when DRAWERS were mentioned, the MUSIC BOX young man was going to draw attention to the fact that his mother was going to be there. One day there were BLACK ONES and she didn't turn up, so I quickly caught on to what he was saying.

The code became more sophisticated as time went on, but they have said that I must not try to put it all in this book as, like a language manual, we must always start with stuff that is easy to understand until we get used to it. But there is a point I must include. When the <u>black</u> drawers turned up, they were saying "NEGATIVE his mother would be there," but when they want to cancel out a NEGATIVE message, they follow it up with another NEGATIVE thing so that it cancels (or negatives) the previous one. They will make me hear some unhappy remark in overheard conversation or other things like when a child will screech. They can know when a child is likely to be overtired or fretful and move me within earshot.

They use this system if I am contemplating buying something that is not good value or warn me if I haven't got enough money in my purse. There is no need for alarm if these overheard remarks in conversation are very depressing. They can make use of everything. The kids are often behind a lot of this.

When there is no external situation that they can use to counteract (negative) a negative thing, a depressing word will go through my head. I can only pick up single words, *very* rarely two or three, unlike DORIS, who could hear sentences, but it is useful to die code at times. They say that it took ten years to train one person and if I don't teach others what I have learned they are

KEEPING A DOG AND BARKING THEMSELVES.

As my gypsy friend has been prone to remark a couple of times recently - and we must 'take note' when things repeat.

As I was checking this page, I picked up a faulty pen. The ink escaped and got onto the page and all over my hands. I knew that I had got something wrong, so duly checked carefully but could find nothing seriously amiss with the writing I went on using the faulty pen and began to wonder if they wanted to leave the story out altogether, but that didn't seem to make sense either. I got up from the divan thing I was sitting on to wash the black stuff from my hands when it dawned. I had been laid up for a day or two with a back problem. It was better that day for the first time but I had been sitting in a bad position, as I realised to my cost, when I got up to wash my hands.

I think the Dimension people must have been trying to do it for centuries and that would explain some of the old superstitions, I bet all the DP groups are chuffed to bits now that someone has pulled it off at last.

Just as I was finishing this ALEX interrupted with a lovely GREEN lettuce he had grown. I said, "Shush I'm trying to concentrate," and he replied, "KNICKERS!"

Poor ALEX. It was the loveliest GREENEST lettuce I had ever seen so I told him so. About this time loads of things seemed to be GREEN, just as had happened once before.

One morning I bought from a store in a jumble town some of those biscuits called HOBNOBS. I put them in a corner at the jumble sale with some other things and went to look at another stall, when I returned, my biscuits had been put out on a table and sold by mistake. I went back to the store and asked for another packet of the HOB NOB type cookies.

On the way home saw a shop called HOBNOBS and after that the expression NOBS for 'you know what'. I was baffled.

The DRAWERS persisted as only our drawers can. CHESTS OF DRAWERS, KNICKERS, BLOOMERS the lot. One jumble morning there were UNDIES GALORE; PINK, BLUE, YELLOW, GREEN, those nylon ones that we used to buy from MARKS AND SPARKS remember? Very pretty. They were all lined up along the table. Someone said 'LIKE A RAINBOW.

I sat down for a cup of coffee when a lady came up to me and said, "ARE YOU THE PERSON WHO HAS BEEN HAVING COINCIDENCE?" and explained that she'd had such lovely experiences and went on to say that her son-in-law in the Dimension had told her how to change a plug. She was puzzled why people didn't understand her though and said, "I FEEL SO SORRY FOR THE REST OF THE WORLD THAT DOESN'T KNOW." (As we all know we must always get a qualified person to check an electric plug if we have had no experience).

Later we had a rainstorm. In between showers the sun was shining so I took a cup of coffee and sat on the doorstep to wait for the postman. ELLA passed by and I remarked, "I'M WAITING FOR A RAINBOW ELLA." But no rainbow materialised until I caught sight of a washing line and there it was; PINK, BLUE and MAUVE. PRETTY COLOURS all in a row.

RAINBOW KNICKERS!

Very resourceful these DP people, aren't they? And that's got to be the understatement of the year. As I said earlier, they have never let me forget it.

Oh dear hysterics! I was a bit apprehensive wondering if I would have to remove this, when a telly dialogue went ...

"DON'T GET YOUR KNICKERS IN A KNOT."

The QUEEN came up again. Lovely films reviewing her troops. THE QUEEN MOTHER too, frequently. Soon after TOPS became prevalent. I had a little WOODEN TOP in the kitchen DRAWER, the TOP one, then a group of WOODEN TOPS in a second-hand shop window. TOPS all the time but I was not impressed. (Think I would have learned by now wouldn't you?) Then the QUEEN again and references to someone named QUEENIE. People kept talking about BISCUITS and the term `TAKES THE BISCUIT'. This is an expression for astonishing.

One day, falling asleep while the telly was on, I was suddenly wakened by the remark, "ITS IN THE TOP DRAWER."

I thought, is the manuscript sample something to do with the QUEEN?

THE NOBS, THE TOPS, THE DRAWERS, OF COURSE! THE QUEEN IS TOP DRAWER! THE

MANUSCRIPT HAS GONE INTO THE TOP DRAWER.

Meaning, that it has gone into the reading file of the TOP CLASS PUBLISHER because it. `TAKES THE BISCUIT.

HOB NOB is an English term for mixing with the upper class.

A couple of days later there was a letter to say that the publisher was interested in the manuscript sample and wanted to see the rest. Opening it the clock struck TWELVE NOON.

One morning while at the kitchen sink a word went through my head quite clearly, `ASTRONOMY".

Shortly after the code came up to warn me that it was going to come back. They used the song

PICK YOURSELF UP

Wondering if I could bear the disappointment, they used another, WHEN YOU WISH UPON A STAR, the words were so comforting.

 LIKE A BOLT FROM THE BLUE, FATE STEPS IN

AND SEES YOU THRU

It was true, the manuscript came back within an hour of the code `tip off. I was very unhappy. The day after it was my birthday. At the market I picked up an old birthday card. On it the words `TO MY DEAR DAUGHTER' so the pain was eased.

That evening, when I was walking down the road

after dark, there was an amazing SHOOTING STAR. It swept across the sky like something from a Disney film. It could have been a satellite burning out, as that may have been easier to predict. After all they probably <u>can</u> see through our telescopes.

So that's why they used "WHEN YOU WISH UPON A STAR"

I felt immediately better and as time went by, they explained that the right time would come when the manuscript will be accepted and that I must be patient for the time being.

There were more clues to bring comfort, among them a piece of music entitled

    I UNDERSTAND JUST HOW YOU FEEL

performed by FREDDIE and the DREAMERS.

Mr father's name is FRED and his companions are the people in the `dream' (the dreamers). There are other clues but too many to include.

Up until the twentieth century and even later in England we had a big CLASS division in the way we lived. Peasantry and class never mixed socially on any large scale so that we always married partners from our own social background.

If a housemaid had loved the young man from the big house and had a baby, it would be unthinkable for it to be brought up in the `class' home. Of course, I know there would have been the odd exception, but generally the babies from such relationships, although probably provided for sometimes, would be brought up in the simpler lifestyle.

The Dimension people tell us that our minds couldn't develop as well as the multi-heritage mind could and this is turning out to be positive. All the people I have come across since, who have been like DORIS STOKES and a friend who is HALF SPANISH and HALF IRISH and can read the manuscript without the backlog problem, are what is generally known as PSYCHIC. I know that the class system provided us with some very clever and beautiful people. Would we and our allies have won the war without it?

In the Victorian era upper class people used to go to the opera and although earlier Shakespeare did write comedies, generally in the nineteenth century the stage stuff was often sad and tragic. Although the music was beautiful, the opera would not have been a lot of help in getting laughter in crowds strong. I know that there would have been exceptions. I am speaking of the majority of stage productions, before the MUSIC HALL and the GILBERT and SULLIVAN comic stuff came along.

When our joy level is raised it increases our awareness of the Dimension people. In the MUSIC HALL DAYS, the seats in the gallery were cheap enough for a poor person to go and it is possible that the Dimension people found that when they were in a laughing crowd they were able to make themselves heard by the subconscious mind.

At the time I was writing this NAT gave me a book on the history of pantomime. I see that it has been with us for a very long time. In the book is a picture of a family waiting for a train after a panto outing. They are clearly definitely not poor people, as the children look very elaborately dressed. It is probable that the psychic tendency was among the poorer people. I think the mixed-heritage was more likely to be in a Gay Nineties audience than earlier in the century and why haven't I thought of this before? On the night that I wrote the document I had spent the day with crowds of happy excited people at the OLDE TYME STREET FAYRE. They all must have had a higher positive level afterwards and I would have been more receptive. That does remind us that the country folk did have the FAIRS and travelling theatre companies so a little recreation must have been had occasionally, even for them but this would have been rare.

Life for everyone was sad though when you think of the child mortality rate and just going to the dentist was an ordeal. No one in any walk of life was very far from tragedy to be able to get their JOY level up enough for the Dimension people to be able to get themselves heard on any vast scale. There may have been one prevailing factor though, which could have alleviated some of it.

With the way we used to marry people from our own backgrounds, the chances were higher than they have been in recent years of marrying OUR right ones as we only mixed with our own class and the lifestyle needs would be more likely to match. It is not surprising that in the past couple of decades this has been a little `thrown´. The Dimension people do say though that we will be more coordinated and our chances of finding happiness much more likely in the future as the help and organising influence is getting more powerful all the time.

The document says
NO ONE WILL HAVE ANY PROBLEM FINDING HAPPINESS IN TIME BUT, AND THIS IS IMPORTANT, WE HAVE TO WAIT UNTIL THE WORLD'S BACKLOG HAS BURNED OUT ...
This could mean that the muddles that we are experiencing now could be explained by the fact that the `info' that is coming from books and telly programmes telling us that we are eternal, is beginning to be understood, and for a time we can't function at our best until our backlog has all gone.

The Dimension people do emphasise the importance of this book not becoming too long, so I have to be careful not to get carried away. But it could be important for us to grasp some simple things.

I'm sure that beautiful music must raise our positive level and anything that we personally enjoy doing must do the same, but there is a high possibility that when we are in a crowd of laughing people, we somehow generate a power that has a healing influence. The time will come when they are able to teach us about this.

When we were rehearsing for our musical shows my friends would lose the tiredness after a hard day's work. The more they laughed, the less tired they became. Laughter seemed to be like a magical healing power and I'm sure that in time they will be able to give us more information.

The higher our misery level is the harder it is for the Dimension people to be able to guide us. I think that when we experience a severe backlog, we can't hear them at all. As the Dimension build up their workforce, they will be able to help us anyway by influencing others around us as they did in the dentists.

COMPASSION on the part of someone can dissolve the effect of a severe backlog when large groups of people pray together, they are conveying COMPASSION probably. The more we understand this is the more powerful the Dimension people's love can be. I am sure that in time they will be able to give us a logical explanation of how it is that some people can actually heal others. I have seen this happen. I do have some ideas that may explain it, but I need to wait to see if some more clues turn up, which they probably will.

One could argue that if they could organise me to be on the road that the young motorcyclist was on, couldn't they have stopped the accident in the first place? The explanation is simple. They would be only too well aware that the boy rides too fast around those lanes. If he has a high misery level then no matter how loud the Dimension people tried to shout out at him to "Watch out! Slow down," even with the intelligence that his age group may well have now, he would not have been able to hear them. Many young people nowadays may have a high misery level when one thinks of how the media is bombarding them with frightening things. Young people are unlikely as a general thing to admit that they are afraid, so it is not surprising to me that they are seeking escape. I don't know how long it will take but sooner or later co-ordination will come and the Dimension people will be able to save us from these things. It is only our ignorance of how it all works that is the cause of so much suffering. There are many programmes that are comforting and educational. People who live on their own would be lost without them, so I am not criticising television generally. I believe no one is to blame for the unfortunate presentations that have a frightening effect. If a presenter has to go into the `thick of it' and into danger to report tragic and depressing news stories, which these courageous people have to do, how can we send help if we don't see it?

When editors have to work on tragic and sad stories it can't do anything else but lower his (or her) JOY level. Unless there is something to raise it again, it is likely to affect their choice of following presentations.

Sooner or later peace of mind will come to everyone and the tendency will change.

The identities go back to about 1915. I think VAN BIENE may have left them and gone full circle but I haven't in this case got anything too solid to substantiate this. They kept on about him a lot with CAVALIERA RUSTICANA and a reference to him too a little while ago published in a book as recently as 1988; THE GREAT CELLOISTS, so they definitely want to tell us something important about him, I wasn't as efficient in deciphering the code then as I am now, so I expect I could have missed clues as well.

They conveniently saw to it that another book was put in one of my "boxes and in it a reference to reincarnation. It contained stories of people who insisted that their dead babies were sent back to them. One was very interesting, well they all were, but this was of a chappie who lost TWO little girls and insisted that the second two were the original little ones. The address where he lives is in the road where I went at first to find the BED and BREAKFAST place on the BRIGADOON TRIP.

So much has come correct that they predicted, that now I have no trouble in believing them. The code becomes more informative each week, so in time they will be able to develop it enough to give us more information as time goes on. Meanwhile, WE'RE NOT COMPLAINING ARE WE?

Some time ago I met a lovely girl who is called a MEDIUM and she said that it all tallies with what she has found out.

In the war when people were transitioning in great numbers there must have been confusion and loneliness. So much misery must have been generated, but now this is all CHANGING. Every time someone joins them the whole thing is different.

More people are there to explain how it's all working and happiness and optimism are stopping the miser}' that was so prevalent before. There has always been people there to explain I expect, but now I think the groups are becoming more organised thanks to the people who have gone before who have had the determination to make us understand enough to last out until their numbers grew stronger and so more powerful.

Just after writing this a psychologist came up on television and he said that when people realise that their consciousness is permanent, they become, in time, compassionate and kind and I think he used the word TOLERANT. Pity we had no video at the time.

The telly coverage one evening was the anniversary of the DAM BUSTERS, the RAF SQUADRON which dropped the bouncing bomb. The next day a friend said he had just got a painting of the DAM BUSTERS' PLANE and A SPITFIRE. The DAM BUSTERS' MARCH MUSIC coming up too.

At a fair the following week we were at a coconut shy when a SPITFIRE swooped down directly over our heads. It was the same one as in my friend's painting. Later at a garden party, I met a lady who told me her husband had been A FIGHTER PILOT in the Battle of Britain. For days after his name came up all over repeatedly and, in my box, that week was a record of the BATTLE OF BRITAIN theme, along with the DAM BUSTERS' MARCH. As I was playing it, just as the music gave a kind of fanfare, a low-flying plane swooped over the house to synchronise. It was then that I wept for the first time; that it should take people so long to accept the Dimension people. After all the patience and struggle they have had to go through to make us know that they are there. BUT THAT WAS SOME TIME AGO.

The main reason for this being, that when our worst fears are stopped, we go into REVERSE, not realising until now that the uncomfortable feeling is only TEMPORARY and NORMAL.

In the document it says ...

`CROSSES HAVE HAD TO BE BORNE´. As well as human sacrifice. I think this is all alluding to the fact that people had to be organised to marry their wrong ones in the hopes that a group of multi-heritage babies would be born, with all the right receiving capability in their minds so that out of all of them, one would have the right genes to be able to pick up the code. Also, the patience they must have had to hand over the plan from generation to generation and keep on and on trying to attract our attention. They were aware of our need for conservation problems during the thirties, even earlier, and the danger we were getting into, so the misery they must have felt in not being able to make us understand must have been a `cross' in itself. Later they were able to give us more information and with it the realisation that ALL IN TIME WILL BE WELL and how all tears will pass and only laughter can remain.

Immediately after I had written the SPITFIRE story, I settled down for a rest and a film of AMY JOHNSON came on. Across the screen go SPITFIRES. In it someone refers to a FLYING VISIT.

The day before I wrote this story, I met the lady who was married to the BATTLE OF BRITAIN PILOT. It was the first time I'd seen her since the garden party. I was on my way to find a card to send to my little grandsons to tell them that we could go on a trip soon, like we did on the day we saw the SPITFIRE swoop down at the fair. As usual I waited for guidance on what kind of card to choose. Then I saw the picture card that would be suitable. It was of a SPITFIRE and, of course, I had my instructions on what the next story must be.

That morning I had tried on a smart white coat at the jumble sale. I didn't buy it, as it was out of date. AMY was wearing the identical one in the old film. They do it all the time, even now though, I miss a lot.

One evening I was thinking I'M MISSING HALF OF IT, just at the same time in a play the dialogue went "YOU'VE MISSED A BIT THERE."

As I write, a film is synchronising and someone is saying to a girl called CONNIE, "SEE WHAT I MEAN?"

When I checked back over this chapter, I saw that

there was no story attached to the DAM BUSTERS. Shortly after, I heard of a retired RAF chappie who had taken part in the DAM BUSTERS' RAID. It could be that they want me to mention the film which was shown of the inventor of the BOUNCING BOMB which was used in the raid and who worked patiently over and over again to get it ready in time, and the inventor of the Wellington Bomber that CLIFF flew.

Later they came up with the explanation for why they wanted to draw our attention to people like this.

ALEX has just come in and said "Good programme on tonight, you know what's his name? The fellow who invented the jet engine."

Footnote: There are books written by AIR CHIEF MARSHALL, LORD DOWDING who was the architect of the BATTLE OF BRITAIN which make references to young pilots who were killed.

One does talk of a young RAF boy who flies with an aircrew so as to guide them. Although Lord Dowding's books are very old, they can still be found in English libraries. They are entitled, MANY MANSIONS and LYNCH GATE, The DAM BUSTERS piano music turned up, on it was a picture of the actor who was in the same outfit as ALEX at the capture of the PEGASUS BRIDGE. The composer was in the same orchestra that my father played in, but not at the same time. And so, they keep going ...

In a BOTANICAL MAGAZINE I saw a wonderful story of how botanists had carefully bred seeds that were descended from the plants that were brought here on the old sailing ships in the last century from the TROPICS. The little plants were getting along nicely in the south of England in large numbers and as that was some time ago, they probably had been taken back to their homeland and planted in the depleted RAIN FORESTS as they grow very quickly, I gather.

I always put my keys in the greenhouse. One day people started to talk about their keys - in the street and at a jumble sale. In a cafe a lady was saying that she forgot her keys so she sat in the GREEN HOUSE. Soon after the song HIGH HOPES came up and it goes THERE GOES ANOTHER RUBBER TREE PLANT. Sure enough, two films in one day about RUBBER TREES. I was really flummoxed with that one as I couldn't see what KEYS had to do with RUBBER TREES.

Soon after in a gardening book was a picture of THOUSANDS of CLOCHES; individual little glass things to put over plants. Green houses kept continually coming in as welt and little faces peeping out of those old-fashioned CLOCHE HATS that we wore in the twenties, together with the song that goes, PEOPLE, PEOPLE WHO NEED PEOPLE and the PEOPLE - TREE and WHAT A WONDERFUL WORLD OF COURSE! KEY PEOPLE! That's it, KEY PEOPLE!

Then the name MITCHELL all the time. MITCHELL?

OF COURSE, the SPITFIRE. R. J. MITCHELL INVENTED THE SPITFIRE! In the thirties or earlier, he was intensely sure that the country was in danger, so, although he was ill, he still kept on getting the spitfire ready and we all know how it saved us.

What the KEYS and CLOCHES were meaning was that all over the world there are people like R. J. MITCHELL who from their school days, or even earlier, have been sought out. Just like little plants under glass and the TROPICAL RUBBER TRFFS in a greenhouse, with their happiness, health and safety watched over carefully because, like R. J. MITCHELL, they have a vital role to play in CONSERVATION, SCIENCE and MEDICINE.

Every time someone joins them, the work force, the power becomes stronger in the Dimension. They are more intelligent than we are and can inspire our subconscious minds with the IDEAS for saving everything and have no problem with working as a team because they have no misery. Now that so many of us are catching on, they are happier than ever before. When we are free from misery, we can't be anything else but constructive in all we do. The world's recovery can't come in five minutes but they say that if we look closely, we will see signs already of hope for the future. It is like the SEA SNAIL that is mentioned in a book illustrated by the WILDLIFE ARTIST who stayed with us, or a BALLOON, slowly drifting all over the world, every month the numbers of happy people in the Dimension will increase and with them POSITIVE POWER.

Soon after I had written this, I heard of a friend who has been offered a wonderful opportunity in CONSERVATION. Oh! That probably explains the reference to `ACTION STATIONS' in the Brigadoon story.

Here we go again, I found it under the piano lid when I wrote this story. Must have been there for years.

One day I decided to leave the bike behind and coach ride. It went around the remote villages and winding lanes for miles. I could see in the distance the hill where I had sung, THE SOUND OF MUSIC. The route took us past the houses where a young lady had lived who had taken part in a professional version of that show and is singing on one of the records that I play. She is in the Dimension now.

As we rode, I was silently singing a tune from the show but not the same one as I had sung before. Over and over it went in my mind.

BUT SOMEWHERE IN MY YOUTH OR CHILDHOOD I MUST I HAVE DONE SOMETHING GOOD

Odd really, also as I thought, totally inappropriate as no way could I think of ANYTHING good that could be attributed to my childhood. That is why I have always had compassion for youngsters who get things wrong, having been there too. I thought surely MARIA'S song would be more appropriate from that show?

♪ SHE'S ALWAYS LATE FOR EVERYTHING EXCEPT FOR EVERY MEAL ... MARIA'S NOT AN ASSET TO THE ABBEY ♫

I knew that if the song persisted it had some meaning though.

As we turned a corner a car came along too fast. How we missed it I don't know, talk about a close shave!

The same thing had happened a couple of days before too. As we carried on our way a beautiful RAINBOW appeared, perfect, complete, like the first one in the field. On our left the hill — clear and lovely but the rainbow was on the opposite side of the bus; I noticed this so didn't get too excited although it was gorgeous. Then, as we rounded a bend slightly, the hill reflected in the bus window and the rainbow appeared to be encircling it. GOSH! It was perfect, like out of a fairy-tale book. The song persisted and persisted.

SOMEWHERE IN MY YOUTH OR CHILDHOOD I MUST HAVE DONE SOMETHING GOOD

On my return a film and in it a pram was running away. It registered a couple of days later when another film portrayed the same thing. Someone catches the pram just in time. OF COURSE! Then I remembered, as a kid I saw a pram racing down the hill. I caught it seconds away from disaster. After the film several others, all with this `just in time' theme. BUT ALL WILL BE WELL, no need to worry, they say. WE ARE IN TIME to save everything, but 'BABY, IT WAS CLOSE!'

What I did notice at meetings of psychic people was that comfort and accuracy would come in 'leaps and bounds' and then there would be an identity that no one knew. The pattern was pretty consistent and odd when so many other things would be accurate. It could be though that this inaccurate information is deliberate on the part of the Dimension people so that our joy capacity isn't overloaded to an uncomfortable level and so we understand about the Dimension gradually. The need for this is going to fade in time as so many of us are being 'broken in' now.

We can see why the meetings were sometimes unpopular as mediums must have often have stopped fears and then the 'backlog' set in next day bringing strange and uncomfortable feelings.

Sometimes when the psychic people end their session, they can be quite tired. I've found too that if I relax and concentrate on the code propped up on a pillow like when we do deep relaxation exercises, it's more comfortable to get up slowly and recover gradually as one can feel quite dazed for a short while. This is normal and can be handled perfectly once we understand it. Actually, lying flat is usually part of relaxation but I find the pillow more comfortable as one hasn't so far to get up, A little gentle hand rubbing and toe wiggling can help speed up the recovery though.

I choose early in the morning to review all the films and events of the previous day, as at that time of day there is little chance of somebody knocking on the door. When this has happened during the times of full relaxation, I have jumped up quickly and found that I would become as `giddy as a goose'. (Although what is there about geese that they are called giddy? All the ones I've come across have been quite bright). Never having suffered from this before I was quite alarmed, but when I checked it out with medical people, they explained that when we are very relaxed all our system is slowed down. If we jump up quickly it takes a little while for it to get going again, so the giddiness was perfectly normal and completely avoidable once we realise that we must just get ourselves going again very slowly. One medical friend said, `Just count ten'. What about a phone? Just turn it off for the time one needs not to be disturbed. I expect this is all common sense to the average person, but I have to make allowances for the fact that I may not be the only person in the world who can be as THICK AS TWO SHORT PLANKS' (although we've probably got to go a long way before we find one).

There has to be a logical explanation for why I can remember events and films of the previous day in a relaxed state and the opposite seemed to apply when I used intense concentration to play the piano and I got the burning face thing and the faster metabolism of the Brigadoon trip. Somehow to intensify my ability to play the piano or write, like after the return from the OLD TYME FAYRE - they have to raise my metabolism, but when I only have to listen and not do anything physical it works better to be totally relaxed. The piano intensity lessened after a time as I became a little more proficient. I daresay that eventually they will be able to explain these things more fully. One thing that they have made clear is that they never push us beyond our limit and they know exactly how much effort we can withstand. So, when I was quite dazed from struggling to play the piano I was subconsciously aware of

DAD saying **"STOP** and RELAX."

They have made it quite clear that they can't take us over. If this was possible, they would have been able to let us know that they were there centuries ago. They can only guide us. Once we understand the reason for these sometimes-uncomfortable sensations, they cease to be a problem.

As the years go by the need to be silent will go too as we become more adept at noticing the code. Some people have had so little practise at being so GLAD that they could sing with JOY, but they will be surprised at how quickly they can learn.

UNCLE GEORGE'S DRINKING SONG AGAIN and references to CHAMPAGNE and CELEBRATION.

JILL had a record. She turned it over several times, on it a picture of the SEA. The word TURN and TERN came up a lot. A recording of TURNER LAYTON the stage artist too. They use everything they can think of and are not fussy about the phonetic spelling.

THE SUMMERTIME THEME kept coming up as the year went on and references in a CHRISTIAN magazine to positive influence growing and the words on the front `THE TIDE is TURNING: One day in a cafe were rows and rows of mugs with names on. There must have been a HUNDRED at least, no exaggeration. As I was looking at them a clock struck TWELVE NOON loud and clear. There were a few people whose identity still hadn't come - GLADYS, sister to TONY and JOY another friend. That day, someone whom I see week after week said, `HELLO GLADYS', (she got my name wrong) and shortly after I saw a sign - `JOY'S RESTAURANT'. The same afternoon of the MUGS, exactly as I was going into my gate a HUGE passenger AIRCRAFT flew slowly past the house and almost straight away another big transporter went across the back. Both of them low, like a FLYPAST.

When I got into the house, I put the telly on. A film was about to start about a chap who was some sort of ANGEL and was supposed to `BLOW HIS HORN AT MIDNIGHT.

It was too far into the story to get the whole plot, but he was in the throes of trying to BLOW HIS HORN before midnight struck and I think the idea was something to do with JUDGEMENT DAY. Anyway, he didn't get to blow it, thank goodness. I switched channels and a girl was singing a song about BLOWING A HORN AT MIDNIGHT. The same theme.

I was reminded of a remark that was made on television about the progressive mess that the world was getting into. It was `IT'S FOUR MINUTES TO MIDNIGHT'. The NOON and MIDNIGHT theme was backed up again, along with THE GOOD OLD SUMMER TIME, and that was MIDSUMMER, the day of the MUGS and the BIG PASSENGER AIRCRAFT. The MUGS had names on, rows and rows of them ... but the chap in the film THE ANGEL, never DID GET TO BLOW THE HORN although it was a close thing.

I think the GOOD OLD SUMMER TIME songs were referring to the time when their numbers would increase to the HALFWAY MARK so that fifty percent of people in the Dimension were involved in the big plan to organise the world's affairs in politics and conservation - people who have had experience in these things and go on being interested in them and influencing them now.

The plans to get a book written accelerated in the last

few years and it does look like there were people in the
TUCKED AWAY VILLAGE who were organised to buy the
houses there so that it would be easier to keep an eye on
them when they transitioned. It was the sort of people they
were that makes me suspicious. Their interests were
CONSERVATION, MUSIC, POLITICS and MEDICINE.
Another knew ROYALTY and another SHOW BUSINESS.
When a well-known politician came in with his identity, he
used a BOX OF HEALTH FOOD PILLS and a lady who
knew ROYALTY was happy with JAM LABELS (as well as
other clues.)

The class distinctions are missing from the
Dimension, not that this lot had any anyway. The
concentration of people who were experienced in matters
that are of the highest importance to world affairs was far
higher than the average.

One day Alex brought home a book on the history of
the little TUCKED AWAY VILLAGE. In it was a picture of
the house where a chappie had lived who was in
intelligence in the war as a CODE BREAKER.

The accent on the GOOD OLD SUMMER TIME kept
going. Obviously, they wanted us to understand that
something of importance was going to happen then.

Immediately after writing this, I decided to pack up
and watch a film. It told of a man who was comforted by
the girl he loved who was in the Dimension. The film was
based on a story that had been written by a lady who used
to visit the TUCKED AWAY VILLAGE. `I think it could be a
reminder that I had made no mention of WRITERS who
lived there.

The world can't do anything else but recover
eventually as the POSITIVE INFLUENCE has OUT

155

NUMBERED THE UNHAPPY people in the Dimension and the whole operation is under control - that was three years before his final writing. No wonder they were talking of CELEBRATION.

One day while playing a record of MERRY ENGLAND (this is a musical based on the days of GOOD QUEEN BESS), it coincided with the Armada's four hundredth anniversary and the south of England celebrated with a repeat of the BONFIRES that were lit at intervals over the country to warn us that the ARMADA of Spanish ships was on its way to invade us. It was defeated and after turning back had to go round our island before returning to its homeland. I don't know why this was, perhaps it was something to do with the TIDES.

My dear old dog DANNY transitioned. I nervously wondered if they would be able to tell me anything about him as he was the first animal to transist since this experience. The next day in bed reading about dogs I heard two dogs barking. They sounded like two friends of his who lived quite two fields away. Had it been Josh's little dog I wouldn't have noticed it the same. Didn't pay much attention and thought if it means anything, they will follow it up with something else. I pulled a piece of paper out from under the music stool where it had got stuck under the leg. It was the picture of a KINGFISHER that I had torn from a book and had been on the mantelshelf when Sheila's letter came with the Conservation Trust picture. Sure enough, in the post again a letter from her enclosing photos she had taken of old DANNY when on their visit. In the photo was a big toy dog in the background - they always like to DOUBLE things when they can. The flash had reflected in his eyes so they just looked like two white stars or jewels, like it does when we look into the camera sometimes with specs.

It must be confusing for transitioned animals at first, as they must wonder why we aren't noticing them, but they get used to it and it must be easier if there is anyone already there that they can recognise, so DANNY will have remembered BELLE his previous owner. They must be able to transmit an image of themselves somehow as they can see each other just as we do.

On the day he left us I went off jumbling as ALEX wanted to be alone for a little while. The jumble sale was for the POPPY appeal. In the queue someone with a dog on a lead called out the name BELLE. Inside the hall, on the windowsill there was a sprig of gypsy heather. It seemed to be all references to my father that afternoon, so I wondered where my mother was.

I managed to be very brave as I knew without a shadow of a doubt that DANNY would be all right and it must be so depressing for the animals in the Dimension to see us crying so much. Of course, his AUNTIE and my mother would have stayed with ALEX with others, to reduce his distress with their compassion and BELLE would have taken DANNY away so that he didn't see his sadness, so I think BELLE and DANNY were in the queue at the jumble sale that day.

A few days later I went to a sale organised by my own loving friends. Someone had decided to get rid of a whole collection of DOG ornaments so there were 'umpteen' all over. At the auction HARRY said, "WHAT AM I BID FOR A DOG CAGE? JUST RIGHT TO TAKE THE DOG TO THE VET." Gone! to that old dog from Y...... Danny came to us from Y........ Everyone was used to

DICKIE – he was well loved by us all!

I ended up with a box of odds. Inside was an ornament of DOUBLE DOGS and the EYES WERE MADE OF SPARKING JEWELS. They sparkled just like the eyes in the photo when they caught the flash.

"DANNY CAN SEE YOU."

Some people mentioned the mushrooms and the fields so I was being reminded to go down where I used to with him. Sure, he'd be coming down there with me to relive memories too.

Much more info came in at a later date, explaining that the DP's can know if a doggie is going to join them. So, if there is no-one that they can recognise, the DP's can speak to a doggies subconscious mind. When they join the Dimension, there will either be a face that they recognise or a voice with which they will be familiar. I know that this is amazing but then so is the whole planet!!

They so far have said that the little doggie personalities only stay in the Dimension for about 2.5 years. That they sleep a lot when not following the personality who they love around. It's a pity that I can't include the story in which they conveyed this info but there is no room to include any more details. When the person who they become attached to has to say goodbye, sadness is experienced but they can still keep an eye on their beloved doggies, who forget them.

Soon after I overheard a conversation in a village hall. A lady was saying that she had lost her little doggie and had just seen one like it. She said he had PUT HIS PAW UP TO HER JUST LIKE HER OWN LITTLE ONE USED TO and added "I FEEL SO SAD."

I could say nothing but so hoped that she would put

two and two together so that the `PENNY WOULD DROP'
as the saying goes, as that is the sort of thing they organise
when checking in an identity for us.

Not long before, the Dimension people had indicated
that the manuscript must be held back for a while. They
used the music THE FOUR SEASONS and GEORGE
FORMBY singing a happy song that synchronised WE'RE
ON THE BEAT, from the film, SPARE A COPPER. Which
was relevant later.

This could have been because other books were
coming onto the market telling us about the Dimension
People and letting the light in, and it was important that this
one must have the right timing. They said that for the time
being (and the seasons came round twice before the `tip off
came to start sending it again) I must be content to wait and
say nothing more to anyone.

They all have their own particular code and one
young lady who had lovely long legs used those telly
advertisements for tights. One has a clock face; the hands
are going round minute by minute and are a pair of long
legs clothed in glamorous tights. When it is repeated, I
know that she is saying something. In one case the remark
that they wished to be recalled was when she used to say...
"THERE'S A REASON FOR EVERYTHING."

The work they must have done to prepare all the
plays and films so that they would follow each one shows
how patiently they have had to wait for the results as some
of the films were made in the thirties. They must have been
planning this way back and were influencing the script
writers long ago.

It was when the lady with the clock tights had come
up again and taking a rest from working on the book, I put

the telly on, a film was about to start. In the cast list was the full name of the lady who was the mother of the baby who was in the pram the day it was saved when I was a child.

The film dialogue that was meant to be noticed was; "ALL IN GOOD TIME, MY DEAR."

They went on to reassure me that they could `MAKE TIME FLY' for which I was truly thankful.

Immediately after writing this the young husband of the lady with the tights came in. He said,

` "CAN'T STOP, NO TIME. THIS IS ONLY A FLYING VISIT."

ALEX asked me why I was laughing. I replied, "Can't tell you now, but will one day," after which, when SHEILA and ROSE asked how the book was getting on, I had to answer, "Just fine," and leave it at that. How puzzling the silence must have been for them.

The great day came when they said it was right to send the book again. It came back with much more encouragement than ever before. I think that in the meantime publishers had received submissions with similar themes and this would have got them used to it so that it was easier to read and assimilate having been `broken in', so to speak.

One day while in the library looking up publishers' addresses, I heard a mother looking for books, she read aloud to her little girl, "HICKORY HICKORY DOCK, THE MOUSE RAN UP THE CLOCK."

I wouldn't have noticed so much if a friend called DICK hadn't been there too, looking at a map and studying with his magnifying glass the SEA.

It wasn't long after that the Dimension people got into OLD SAILING SHIPS again and so often, they were coming into harbour. (DOCK).

Every single day from then on, a clock would strike. These ranged from BIG BEN on radio and telly ads; to our own TOWN CLOCK.

Meanwhile the identities kept up a steady stream. PADRE JONES who was VICAR at the CHURCH in the TUCKED AWAY VILLAGE was able to tell us that he knew all about those ARUM LOLLIES. he had given us to give to my mother in hospital. We thought they were too formal so we hid them in a cupboard and forgot them. This was when I lived with ROSE.

It was one of those things that she and I talked of when we met again. PADRE was once in charge of a little church in ROMANIA where he knew QUEEN MARIE long ago. He had personal letters and photos of her, so I know it was true. I believe he was the inspiration behind the little book I found in which there was the information about the ROMANY'S being taken for slaves in ROMANIA.

During the time Padre's identity was coming in earlier in the year. I'd taken off to an evening jumble and parked the bike outside a church. As I looked up at the door, the street lighting seemed to outline the magnificence of its Gothic stonework. The sky was clear and sparkling with millions of stars and was so beautiful I was still thinking of it when I got home and put the tape recorder on. Immediately the song THE HOLY CITY. The words tell of `I SEE A TEMPLE THERE' and go on to tell of a dream that one day all will be well with the world.

After writing this I stopped for a rest and put the telly on when a dialogue went "THE HOLY CITY IS ONCE MORE IN CHRISTIAN HANDS," and went on to talk of ARMISTICE to the strains of the song THERE'S A LONG

LONG TRAIL, A WINDING meaning I think that the NEW
JERUSALEM that the song refers to will take them a little
time.

Some children were playing with a YO-YO. This is a
TOP that is manoeuvred up and down a piece of string, and
very expert they were too! Its success depends on balance.
The Yo-yos were repeated another day by more children
who knocked on my door to show me.

At the cheese market I asked for three quarters of a
pound. She cut a piece which weighed exactly right and
gave me ONE PENNY in change. Someone called her name.
"MARGERY."

Meanwhile a telly game came up. The presenter
remarked about all three contestants being called John. In a
film shortly after there were THREE JOHNS in the captions
all together. The MARGERY name again too.

In the health food shop, they were short staffed so we
had to wait for quite a while. I had time to study all the pots
of natural medicines on the shelf. Some were called NEW
ERA. When we arrived at the counter the assistant
apologised and did the same thing as MARGERY did with
the weight, and gave me ONE PENNY in change.

I have some lovely friends who travel like gypsies
do. They are keen on conservation, natural medicines and
organic food. Their concern for the earth has led them to
peaceful campaigns against cruelty to farm animals and the
positive things all so important to our future. The hippies as
they were dubbed were responsible for knocking out the
class distinctions in England in the seventies and so many of
their children will have the new-intelligence as they must be
multi-heritage.

There was a trailer for sale. Some people were

standing on both ends, among them a beautiful MOTHER-TO-BE dressed in the traveller style. The far ones stepped off so it started to go down on the young girl's side. There was no problem, it just went down taking her with it.

The Dimension people wanted her to represent the FUTURE. They went on to explain that now that the Dimension people are working together on such a big scale, they will, in time, be able to `PHONE IN COMFORT to our subconscious mind. That when we lose a loved one, we will somehow be able to manage in a way we weren't able to in the past. This will become more powerful as time goes on.

The time will come when future generations will be able to hear the actual voice, but before then the knowledge that they are safe will have come and this is going to start altering our physical health and the decisions we make. For instance, the need to smoke will not be so intense. So much illness will be avoided that way. Doctors in the Dimension will be able to inspire Doctors here with new ideas, as their intelligence is ahead of ours.

Of course, `ALL WILL TAKE TIME', as they colourfully pointed out `ROME WASN'T BUILT IN A DAY'

All the same it isn't going to take hundreds of years either. It just stands to reason doesn't it?

The old rhyme goes

SEE SAW MARGERY DAW JOHNNY SHALL HAVE A NEW MASTER HE SHALL HAVE BUT A PENNY A DAY BECAUSE HE CAN'T WORK ANY FASTER.

I must learn to be patient like in the health food shop queue. THE NEW ERA WILL COME, THE NEW JERUSALEM, when all will know with absolute certainty that we are eternal. They were able to explain why it CAN'T GO ANY FASTER and only here and there can the PENNY DROP for the time being.

The young mother represents the FUTURE and they are telling us that the BALANCE IS ON HER SIDE, and THE TIDE IS TURNING IT IS NO LONGER FOUR MINUTES TO MIDNIGHT THE ARMADA THAT THREATENED THE WORLD HAS TURNED BACK THE DIMENSION IS IN CHRISTIAN HANDS And WHEN THE MULTI-HERITAGE COMES THE WORLD WILL HAVE A NEW MASTER. SNAIL SHELLS kept turning up. I found a huge one in the field. Odd that, it was like those snails that the French use in their cooking. How on earth did it get there? ALEX came in with a bag of SEASHELLS.

I shoved one in my pocket along with a shiny tiny sword, it must have come from some toy. The sword exactly fitted inside the shell. I had once said to the lady in the big house, "THE WORLD'S MY OYSTER AND WITH MY SWORD I'LL OPEN IT." Thinking about it now it could be a fitting slogan for the PEOPLE FROM THE TUCKED AWAY VILLAGE.

The children are playing an essential part. They are far more intelligent that when in this dimension. Whether this is because they can see everything from a clearer view point or whether it is just that their minds are unhampered by anything unconstructive and they are free from any sort of misery. It stands to reason that when our lives are serene, and this is inevitable once we are fully aware of the comfort of knowing that all is well with our loved ones, unhampered as we will be for the first time in mankind's history by the mystery we will then make better decisions. It's just common sense that our own intelligence will improve. Our misery level must get lower just with that problem removed from our minds. The Dimension has always been there first so it stands to reason that their intelligence is going to be better than ours. Even the simplest things will count, for instance, for the first time in my life I've stopped biting my nails as I no longer have misery - the doctors who said that that was a tension symptom had it right. In fact, it's marvellous when we think just how many things they <u>have</u> got right, in spite of the mystery that people have had to live with.

So much credit must be given to people in history who have been willing to suffer for mankind's sake like the religious martyrs with their teachings of faith. They saved it all because they stopped our misery level enough to keep the balance above the danger level generally. The children are numerous now. DORIS had a wall covered with photographs of children who had been able to contact their parents.

Tiny babies just doze and I think they could be first in line for the 'return trip'. The more excited and interested they are, the more awake they stay. They've explained that they can sleep sometimes. Mind you, the Dimension people do say that with the invention of the TELEVISION and its ability to depress thousands of people in one go, and so lower their joy level on such a vast scale, they had to get their thinking caps on smart-ish as at the rate it was going, mankind would not have survived till the new mind came naturally. 'BUT ALL WILL BE WELL NOW, they say.

The children grow up so that by the time this book is on sale these original ones will be mature and they will have trained others to take their place before they move on to more grown-up things.

I'm sure that they will be keeping track of the present lot though. The fact that the children mature when in the

Dimension has been backed up by psychic people.

Footnote:

The television programmes have begun to come up with some very positive stuff, DANCING ON ICE, SO YOU THINK YOU CAN DANCE, and others like this are filling a lot of television time now, so my optimism that the turning point is not far away is not unfounded. I did laugh, too, at the lovely series of POP STAR TO OPERA STAR, after all, I had said about the OPRAH in the early nineteenth century; but this is twenty-first century, people singing it and I was delighted to see that it was the happy songs that got people's votes. I think others will see sooner or later a turning point in the world's affairs. Much to their surprise.

OH, I nearly forgot, there was the programme- OVER THE RAINBOW as well.

In the beginning the kids used to come in when there were carnations on the cafe tables. As we progressed, they used all sorts of things. One day went to see NAT, he was at church. I was surprised as they organise us so they wouldn't have wasted my time without a reason, no matter how small the reason is, as tiny things count for something too. Sitting on the step I noticed a big CARNATION in a pot. In the breeze it brushed my face.

One day when SYLVIA was out with her dogs, she found a cheque book with a signed cheque in a BREAD bag. She took it to the police station. On her way home the collie found a BREAD ROLL in the litter bin.

About that time SYLVIA was having a hard time and she couldn't have any sort of little treat. She has a twenty-two (or thereabouts) inch waist and is about five feet, so doesn't suffer, as I do, from a surfeit of cream cakes. A few days after the cheque incident there was a lady at her door holding a box of chocolates and a bunch of CARNATIONS and was so thankful for the cheque book.

Not long after, the baby girl in the Dimension from the FRUIT AND VEGETABLE SHOP was joined by her mummy. Straight away her identity came in. A film so obviously his check in.

When an old friend of ours checked in <u>her</u> identity, she used her surname, the brand of a famous GLOVE FIRM. The advertisement had a picture of a HAND HOLDING A GLOBE. We had sung the song in our shows.

HE'S GOT THE WHOLE WORLD IN HIS HANDS HE'S GOT THE LITTLE. TINY BABY IN HIS HANDS And the song IF YOU'RE HAPPY, CLAP YOUR HANDS.

I can now hear the strains coming from the telly of some children singing IF YOU'RE HAPPY AND YOU KNOW IT CLAP YOUR HANDS. OH DEAR, THEY ARE POINTING OUT THAT I'VE MISSED A BIT OF THE SONG, HAVEN'T I?

The daddy's identity came in for days. In the film they used the other song as well that we had sung and it was in the same order. No mistaking the message of JOY.

The globe has "HEAVEN SCENT" on it and the gloves have tiny faces on each finger.

The kids' WINDMILLS came up frequently afterwards, it's a pity they can't all go in this book.

This entry was made later...

In the original notes I had a lovely little story about a MOUSE. One made his home in our PIANO. At night I used to hear a funny little noise as he ran along the strings.

Everyone laughed and someone referred to the words of a song we had used in CINDERELLA

     A MOUSE WITH CLOGS ON ...

From the song A MOUSE LIVED IN A WINDMILL

I was astonished when his little identity came in when he went into the Dimension. I didn't include it in the book but this must have been disappointing to whoever thought to make one of us leave a door open knowing that some crumbs had been dropped on the floor, (or something of the sort) I bet the kids thought that one up, so I have made amends.

When I got the typewriter out to settle down and retype this, ALEX called me from the sitting room "COME IN HERE QUICKLY OR YOU'LL MISS 'FLOG IT."

This is an antique programme so I went in to please him but I did want to get on, The presenter was studying a little automated toy. It was a little band of MICE and one was PLAYING A PIANO.

This second reference to a mice band probably could have been because some people think of mice as negative so to be on the safe side they have used two.

Photo courtesy of DUKES of DORCHESTER

Before my experience in SCOTLAND there was a news item on the local telly station about a young boy of thirteen (or fourteen) who was terminally ill and had only a few months to go. He was wearing a peaked cap. He had expressed a wish to ride in a POLICE CONTROL CAR. His wish was granted and the telly news sent a cameraman. The presenter probably didn't want the assignment, poor chap, but the skill in which the young boy handled the situation was still more evidence of the new intelligence that is on its way.

The Dimension people can intensify our memory and even though the programme was only a few minutes, I can remember the lovely face as though it was yesterday. When there was a tragedy on the telly, the identities came up frequently. When, more than one was lost they let one identity-come in so that we could assume that all were safe. They used the most convenient name, like a young man called CRISP, for instance. So, CRISPS came up in conversation or boxes of odds. They always checked something in. After a while they stopped doing this, I think because they know that we will now take it for granted.

I couldn't remember them all though, even if I wrote five books, but the identity of the young boy who rode in the POLICE CAR never came up. I wondered if it was just that we could take it for granted as I had been so impressed by his personality. I did so wish that it would though.

One Friday I went off for a day out on the bus. At a bus stop a boy was wearing a peaked cap - on it a PAIR OF CLAPPING HANDS. I didn't register until a little while later when another boy got on aged about thirteen and wearing the identical cap (it didn't have the hands though). His companion began to whistle. Then the boy in the cap took up the song.

HE'S GOT THE WHOLE WORLD IN HIS HANDS
HE'S GOT THE LITTLE TINY BABY IN HIS HANDS!

Then the bus passed the television studio that the programme came from about the young boy. Waiting on the side of the road was a POLICE TRAFFIC CONTROL CAR.

Two days after, I saw a young boy in a van, the resemblance unmistakeable! HE WAVED HAPPILY TO ME and in my mind, I said LOVE YOU TOO DARLING.

The latest record is playing now – THREE WISHES.

Now if I'm not mistaken, I can guess what the other two are and being the smart young man, he is there won't be much we can tell his MUM and DAD.

Last Sunday an old friend whom we haven't seen for ages pulled up outside my gate and asked to sec ALEX. He was accompanied by a young boy and was keen to get to know all the kids, being a COPPER. The car was a POLICE TRAFFIC PATROL CAR.

As I am typing this in the kitchen, I can hear the telly in the next room. The programme is THE BILL (English slang for police). When I have been worried and anxious the kids have reminded me frequently `WERE ON THE BEAT, and the answers have come.

The peaked cap became very common later but when this was written there weren't so many about. Also, the same thing applied to the MUGS that had the names on. And OH DEAR! It has become fashionable for people to wear their hair tied back like CINDERELLA when the MOUSE took the BLUE-RIBBON out of the drawer for the BLUE BIRDS, in the Disney version.

Now doesn't that have a familiar ring?

They want us to notice mirrors.

If someone is talking of some unhappy experience or illness, if a MIRROR is nearby, we have to REVERSE the simple warning. They don't have to be reflecting in it as long as one is nearby. If the word REFLECT or REFLECTION is used in conversation this counts as ONE.

171

So, when the hill with the rainbow REFLECTED in the bus window, they had to counteract the OPPOSITE way round message in some way.

On the day of the ride round the hill I hadn't learned about the MIRRORS so I didn't register as I would now, whether the coach had one or two in my sight-line. Two would cancel out the first. I called to mind the time that the hills were reflected in a bus window in the film THE SOUND OF MUSIC so the first reflection cancelled out the REVERSE in the second. There was no rainbow in the film, it was only the hills that were in reverse on the bus ride round where I had sung THE SOUND OE MUSIC that day with such joy.

I have never known them to use a MIRROR to reverse a positive remark and when I have noticed a positive happening like the reflected hills there is always something to counteract the reversal.

The reference to THERE GOES ANOTHER RUBBER TREE, PLANT which tells the story of a little ant who eats his way through a RUBBER TREE until it falls, has actually got at first sight, a negative theme. The reference earlier to YOU'VE GOT TO BE "CAREFULLY TAUGHT, also has the same tendency so I think that as the first song is from the musical SOUTH PACIFIC where the RUBBER TREE grows, then one negative song will reverse the other.

Also, the one that FRED ASTAIRE sings in

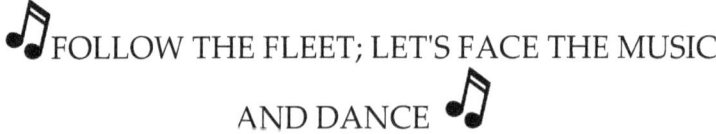

FOLLOW THE FLEET; LET'S FACE THE MUSIC AND DANCE

172

has an unhappy theme. It bothered me a bit, so I replayed the video which I found shortly after the telly film and the part where FRED is getting ready to go on stage to perform the number.

Just before he was handed the DRESS SHIRT by his Chief Petty Officer friend, FRED had been looking in his MIRROR. The BLUE ROSE story has a MIRROR too and the RED LAMPSHADE one features a REFLECTION, both were followed by explanations but there is no room here to record them (BILL'S big brown jug too.) It is important that the code is not made too complicated, we need to understand the basics, the rest will come with experience.

You can bet on it that your loved ones will want to get `in on the act' sooner or later. Most of us live busy lives, so do the DP's. Lots of us will be content just to know that they are safe and happy.

The motorbike boys in the Dimension come with me on the bike and the group is becoming enormous, but they have a tremendous amount of work to do. No one is having time to `sit and stare'. The kids adopted ROLLS for their code so when people start talking continually about BREAD and the BAKER as they are passing in the street or on a bus, or in shops, I know that the kids are on duty and are guarding us.

When they are excited and happy about something, they use the song THE MUFFIN MAN THE MUFFIN MAN.

A few days after I heard from BOB I was at the auction when BALLS kept rolling into me. It was the children's half term from school and I didn't register until quite a time after how many times that morning I had been BUMPED with a ball. Our Dimension kids were there as the `just missing each other' kept going and people said "SO

SORRY", far too frequently to be accident. Of course, it is hilarious. I have to just laugh out loud sometimes, can't contain it.

I found some BREAD ROLLS still in their wrappers that had been thrown away so I took them home for SYLVIA'S dogs. She has a COLLIE and a SCOTTIE; the kids' code came up when some children were playing with a tea set that they had found in a box. The Dimension kids use BLUE and WHITE, china as their code too, but the story of how they started this is too long to include. They started with DUTCH DELFT. I should have taken more notice on the day of the balls than I did.

After BOB'S visit I was walking by the railway track when a train came along, it made a terrible noise stopping and starting and rocking and rolling. I thought salt pots would be shaking for sure and hoped people in the houses it passed had double glazing. I saw someone with two dogs, they were a SCOTTIE and a COLLIE, further on I passed a house. A lady with a SCOTTIE exactly like the one I had just seen was in the garden, a tin of dog food in her hand. She said...

"I FOUND THIS ROLLING AROUND IN THE BOOT OF THE CAR."

We had a little chat and when I went back up the road saw the SCOTTIE and the COLLIE again. It was days before I `twigged' it, even though I had bought a tin of SALT that had rattled and rolled round my top box that day, and SYLVIA has a SCOTTIE and a COLLIE.

The Dimension kids were responsible for getting me to understand the word ROLL. I was supposed to say in the notes SHAKE RATTLE AND ROLL. (Faggot story remember?) I had missed their word.

I got better at it in time, now they go `hammer and tongs' as the saying goes. I am sure that if I hold on long enough others will notice these things, then we will be able to all laugh together.

A song came up from a musical

WE NEED A LITTLE XMAS and goes on about

 SLICING UP THE FRUIT CAKE

AND TINSEL AND THE CHIMNEY

Xmas had crept up on me, only a few days to go when I realised that I had made no preparations. The notes on the coincidences were raking hours and hours and even then, I couldn't keep pace with them. I wrote that I didn't know how the dickens I was going to be ready.

I got some flour and fruit and threw in some eggs and sugar and shoved it in the oven. Couldn't believe my eyes when I went to look - PERFECT! Exactly like KATIE used to send round before she went into the Dimension. All very suspicious!

The house seemed to get Itself in order, I was amazed at how quickly all the muddles got sorted. I went off to the supermarket on the afternoon of XMAS EVE and with twenty minutes to go before closing time I remembered that I didn't have any frill to put round the cake, I ran around the shops but they were all sold out and with FIVE minutes left, returned to the supermarket. A little girl bumped me with a baby buggy and as I turned around, she did it for the second time. I suddenly had the idea to ask the young lady on the cash desk if she would sell me the GOLD and

SILVER tinsel decorating the till. And, for a few pennies she let me have it. It looked marvellous, very shiny and bright. When I got home, I played the record my father must have organised for me THE GOLD AND SILVER WALTZ

I didn't record the GOLD and SILVER STORY so in the newspaper was the headline in HUGE letters, an advertisement for **GOLD AND SILVER**

The kids weren't going to let me forget a third time (or was it four times?) The fun and nonsense that they got up to all the rest of the holidays!

WELL! There's no need for me to worry that I can't record it all here, as it's only a matter of time before YOU'LL BE HAVING XMAS GREETINGS OF YOUR OWN. I hope it won't be summertime before you catch on though, I had sent RON a record. The song went... IT'S BEGINNING TO LOOK A LOT LIKE XMAS. SOON THE BELLS WILL START

And it goes on to refer to a CAROL IN OUR HEARTS, meaning that EVERYONE will have a SONG IN THEIR HEARTS when they know that the Dimension people are there and SOON THE BELLS WILL START

Every single day since then, XMAS is mentioned by something or someone. As I am correcting this, ALEX has just interrupted to say that he's fixed the XMAS fairy lights.

RAY, the postman, (of the little dog story) does a SANTA CLAUS for a charity organisation. One day he asked me if I could find a HANDBELL in my auction travels. SYLVIA has a tiny old world cottage with funny little staircases and oak beams in the ceiling. One evening we were sitting by her fire with its inglenook when we were examining RAY'S SANTA CLAUS outfit. It was ages before I registered that SYLVIA was wearing a bright red velvet trouser suit at the time.

In the dining room there was an old-fashioned Victorian fire place. She couldn't use it as the chimney needed repairing. With the house being four hundred years old, it's not surprising that it is expensive getting it into perfect condition to sell. The rain was coming in the roof around the chimney. Poor SYLVIA worried stiff about the effect of damp and how she could afford to get it repaired. GLEN was then far away down south and anyway; she didn't want to take his time now that he was working so hard.

One day at a jumble she bought some brass wall lights. I didn't think too much of them, but then I'm not an expert on these things. I took them to an art dealer and he, to my surprise, took the lights for auction. When the day dawned, went off to the sale. Just overhead a BIG PLANE was flying across a clear blue sky. Going into the sale a girl came by eating a BREAD ROLL and was wearing the identical shoes to SYLVIA'S granddaughters. The lights that cost one pound got a HUNDRED AND TEN POUNDS!

After she had recovered from the shock, SYLVIA had to think about how she could get the work done. She was hesitant about alarming GLEN about the chimney as he was working so hard at building up a new life bricklaying, singing in a ROCK BAND and PLAYING GUITAR, so she didn't want anything to interrupt that.

She was sitting in the armchair by the fire when SYLVIA noticed an advert in the weekly paper. It was for CHIMNEY REPAIRS. Just after she noticed a newspaper on the floor, the sports page uppermost and the headline shot *out* at her `COME ON GLEN'. So, she decided to tell him about the damp after all, to find that for two weeks during the Christmas holidays he would have no work to do as his firm was closing down. So, GLEN said he would come home for a couple of days.

One evening on the telly someone was talking about selling FIREPLACES and TWO references to MUGS. So, I thought BETTER RING SYLVIA co see what's up. She said "SO GLAD YOU RANG CON. I'M LONGING TO TELL YOU; GLEN HAS DONE THE CHIMNEY TODAY. WE'VE JUST LIT A FIRE. IT'S SMASHING." She was so excited, all anxiety over the damp gone.

The current record is going

 BY THE FIRESIDE

This was recorded by JESSIE MATTHEWS who was on the same bill as SYLVIA when she was in the travelling theatre.

The clock continued to strike each day — on the television, in books, in the town, unfailingly. After a time, the clock is followed by HELLS. Often the clock first and then sooner or later during the day BELLS — church bells, hand bells, All kinds of bells. And I met DAVID on his way to church; BELL practise.

AUNT DAISY came in with the MIDSUMMER theme again and uses the record of the musical... THE BELLS ARE RINGING

When she lived in the city of London, her little flat she shared with UNCLE GEORGE was situated at the top of a high building in an alley. The echoes of even" sound could be heard clearly, although they were seven hundred or so steps up and she reassures us that the `bells really are

ringing' when the music goes

 ALL AROUND THERE'S THE SOUND OF
THE MIDSUMMER'S NIGHT BELLS IN THE AIR ARE
RINGING EVERYWHERE. I CAN HEAR FOOTSTEPS
THAT PASS ON THE STREET

In one song on the record AUNT DAISY is actually
reminding me that I owe her daughter-in-law a thank you
phone call. All the songs on that record are relevant but
along <u>my</u> street can be heard the sound of the ice cream
man and his little tinkling tune I'M POP EYE THE SAILOR
MAN just as I had finished trimming round a sailing ship
photo to include. So, hint taken and must resist the
temptation to put it all in the book.

Hold on a bit! Mustn't get too enthusiastic with the
trimming. A song that should be mentioned from that show
could be

JUST IN TIME

From the top of AUNT DAISY'S building could be
seen many famous LONDON LANDMARKS. It was only
weekdays that I spent there but I'm sure that Sunday must
have produced so many church bells. No wonder they are
on about ORANGES AND LEMONS SAY THE BELLS OF
ST CLEMENTS.

The music "DAISY BELL", "TWO ON A TANDEM"
and "WE ALL HAVE A SONG IN OUR HEARTS" turned

up at this time.

Isn't St Clements the memorial church to the Royal Air force and to Lord Dowding KEYS GREENHOUSES and SPITFIRES were all over the place again. A lovely film with EROL FLYNN as a captain of a sailing ship in the time of GOOD QUEEN BESS determined to make her see the importance of forming a fleet of ships to fight the ARMADA, that he was sure was out to invade us. With his fellow sailors he got marooned in a swamp and was successful with his sword in hacking his way through a tropical forest out into freedom and light.

RUBBER TREES too and the PEOPLE WHO NEED PEOPLE song going through my head, I had no idea what they were on about but knew it was something for sure.

I got to know the little grandmother. Besides the songs from WILD VIOLETS she uses the old rhyme ONE, TWO, BUCKLE MY SHOE and when the colour PURPLE turns up, I know she has something to say.

It is twelve and a half years since the rainbow in the field. Shortly after writing it up that day, everything started to turn GREEN. We have a lovely friend who is in the Dimension. She had red hair and so often used to wear that colour.

I had written to GERALD, her husband, to say that "LILLY uses GREEN." A couple of days later I saw him sitting in his garden. The entire lot was LAWN. He had turned the whole garden GREEN.

LILLY, ANNA, ROSE, VIC and ALEX had gone to school together in the tucked away village. ALEX said that first CHRISTMAS, "LILLY was a LOVELY GIRL BUT SHE USED ALWAYS TO BE LATE." I had to giggle when her Christmas greeting came in. She left it until halfway through JANUARY!

It also has just dawned on me that LILLY'S GREEN completes the RAINBOW. DAD'S RED, ADELE'S BLUE, DAISY'S ORANGES AND LEMONS, my MOTHER'S LILAC and GRANDMOTHER'S VIOLET.

Soon after writing this I walked down the lane. It had been raining and `be blowed' if there wasn't ANOTHER RAINBOW stretching across the same field, beautiful as though it was painted! I met some people who could see it too. It became more lovely and began to DOUBLE like they do.

On my return ALEX came in and said "I BET YOU DIDN'T NOTICE I'VE MOWED THE LAWN."

After this they turned to all things NAUTICAL. References to the COASTGUARD (who influenced RON to go into the NAVY) LIGHTHOUSES and a LIFEBOAT COXSWAIN who lived near us when we were on the East Coast and how they have to have `ALL HANDS ON DECK' and so many old SAILING SHIPS in full sail GLIDING CONFIDENTLY INTO THE FUTURE.

The light houses reminded me of BILL; it is ages since I wrote his story. But a programme came up with the jockey in his painting. He talked of "getting near the winning post."

Could it be that BILL is saying that a publisher will have ROOM FOR ONE MORE and he will no longer have to keep reminding me, as he often does, to WALK DON'T RUN.

WE ARE SAILING WE ARE SAILING

Confidently into the FUTURE all in the SAME DIRECTION as the sailing ship in `TWO YEARS BEFORE THE MAST. Altogether there were eight.

After I had written this people became obsessed with their carrots. ALEX brought a <u>huge</u> one in and told me I must look out for that giant DUTCH seed again.

In the street there were two young people, one dressed as a DUTCH BOY, his companion as ANDY PANDY, collecting for charity.

I was reminded of the day when I saw the clocks with the faces and how they were like the clock that I had painted for the kitchen in our production of CINDERELLA.

In a supermarket there was a huge consignment of carrots. I'd never seen so many carrots in my life. They kept up the theme day after day, so of course, no doubt about it, the kids were on about <u>something.</u>

On the telly, someone said, "YOU ARE HARD

WORK SOMETIMES." This was not said impatiently as they always have understanding for us and know that we will catch on in time as they aren't going to let up until we do.

Some months ago, I saw a friend whose son had gone into the Dimension. I longed to tell her of the code, but the Dimension people indicated that I must hold it back for a while. So, I told her to "HOLD ON" and "LATER IN THE YEAR WE WILL HAVE A LAUGH TOGETHER." I am now hoping that it will not be long before I can discuss it with her as I see her at the auctions regularly.

Yesterday we talked of the electricity generating WINDMILLS and how they are harmless to the environment and are giving us hope of new ideas to get power from natural sources. I said, "When we see them, they are saying `HOLD ON WE'RE COMING'

The week before I had found a record and being without glasses, I'd asked her to read the title for me. It was SHAKE, RATTLE AND ROLL. Yesterday, to remind me again, a film with the song SHAKE, RATTLE AND ROLL. Of course, there has to be a link and I am hoping chat I've got this one right.

I said to my friend "IT WON'T BE LONG NOW," meaning that I could give her COMFORT before long and soon after seeing her I overheard a bit of a conversation in the cafe and the words HEAVEN SENT. I came home with THICK CUT BREAD, by mistake. Could it be that I have left out one of the children's words again? Should it have been HOLD ON WE'RE COMING SOON?

And means

HEAVEN SENT COMFORT IS COMING <u>SOON.</u>

After I had written this, ANNA came in and said about how she had prepared the CARROTS for a church dinner party for FIFTY people.

As I was checking this page ALEX came in and said "I'VE JUST HEARD THEY ARE TALKING OF PUTTING AN ELECTRICITY GENERATING WINDMILL ON" and he named the farm where I had seen the RAINBOW IN THE FIELD.

And on the BRIGADOON anniversary this year the sun shone like it's never done before on the PICTURE.

Soon after, Carnival time again. The fairground people arrived in each town with the MERRY-GO-ROUNDS and CAROUSELS. One day our bus was held up while a fairground vehicle REVERSED into a FIELD. The weather turned bad. All the same the parades carried on although it was a miracle that they weren't all blown away.

One night decided to walk down to SYLVIES. She had been wet through twice that day with the dogs so had to give her a hand with their evening walk.

The weather was awful, so had planned to catch a bus back up. As I walked cars came along and swished water all over me. I laughed when the bus didn't come, so started to walk up the hill, scarf blowing away and umbrella inside out, fighting the storm every inch of the way. Even a bit rough for me!

Early next morning woke to a clear sky, two stars shining and a silvery glow on the horizon heralding a full SUNRISE.

Birds were chippering in the garden, reminding me of films recently with references to LARKS and so many people named BILLY. All the leaves had gone and the brilliant light shone on the picture lighting up the embroidered background. A perfect GOLDEN SKY.

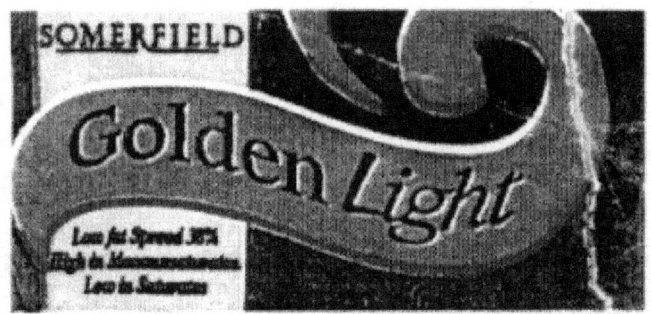

The name SOMERFIELD is relevant

The name SOMERFIELD is relevant

ALEX started to fuss about the string that was holding the picture of JESUS. He said he was afraid it would fall. It looked OK to me but to please him I took it down and replaced it with something stronger. When it was put back up it was hanging slightly lower and at the time, I was aware that this would alter the sunlight patch on it. I knew though that it was impossible to repeat the framed effect of that first year as the window frames are inches deeper so the panes are smaller.

The book was returned so many times that my faith was beginning to fade. I sleep in the room with the picture and at dawn in the spring I keep the little top window open so that I can hear the birds' chorus.

One day they were silent, not a cheep could I hear. For the first time ever in the morning I opened the casement. Lo and behold! When the dawn sunlight appeared I was astonished to see that the oblong of light exactly fitted the picture. The figure central and quite beautiful. I thought, surely it must mean something special after all. Why hadn't I ever opened the casement before? I photographed it and saw that the name of the town where it was processed is a SHIPPING DOCK.

Could it be that my SAILING SHIP is coming into PORT, and will there be others to share the PRECIOUS LOAD.

At the same time a very old schoolgirl's book turned up. Because of copyright integrity I cannot include a picture. In it was depicted a piece of music and included in the title was ME

These books were an identity check in. They have the full name of a friend in them, whose name is JOHN and is part of the SEE-SAW MARGERY DAW STORY

Note TWO MARGERYS.

♪ THESE ARE A FEW OF MY FAVOURITE THINGS ♪

Can't put them all in. If we did we would be the size of the ENCYCLOPAEDIA BRITANNICA and we would need a lorry to carry it around. This lot don't believe in doing anything by halves do they?

A lovely book turned up recently about the QUEEN MOTHER,' entitled CROWN JEWEL. It is published by BLOOMSBURY. I took it to a bookshop to be sold and when I called in later found it was gone.

In the telly episode of CORONATION STREET, a young lady said that her cat was missing. It turned up again and this is one of those times when I didn't see the connection for a few days, so I wish I could be absolutely sure that I have remembered the dialogue correctly. I think it went, "WHERE HAVE YOU BEEN?"

Very shortly, almost simultaneously, the EASTENDERS had a cat missing too. This is an English series that is like CORONATION STREET shown several times a week and is set in the EAST END of LONDON. They too used the expression, "WHERE HAVE YOU BEEN?" when it returned.

There are always hard-working and colourful people at the market town. Overhearing a conversation in the shop, I pricked up my ears as you can imagine. "THE QUEEN BE A-COMIN' ON A VISIT," and the old farmer named the ABBEY TOWN.

About this time an advertisement appeared. It featured a tiny dancer, the resemblance to SYLVIA striking. She ran and danced merrily over the ROOF-TOPS and CHIMNEY POTS and was dressed in a PUSSY CAT costume.

I forgot it though, when a couple of days later I went down to see her but found her out. Next day I said "WHERE'D YOU GET TO SYLVE?"

She replied, "I'VE BEEN TO SEE THE QUEEN."

When a play came on, I didn't realise even when someone was bidding at an auction and said, "THIS IS MY FIELD." HEAVENS! I remember now PANDY, (ANDY PANDY, THE BLACK AND WHITE CAT) he went `missing too, only to return safe and sound later. How could anyone be so slow? I deserve to eat THICK CUT BREAD for the rest of my life.

The PUSSY CAT, PUSSY CAT, WHERE HAVE YOU BEEN? story. THE QUEEN IS THE MANUSCRIPT! And could be someone's FIELD! That will explain the influx of

TIDDLY WINKS games that turned up at that time. There were other clues too, too numerous to mention like SHOOTING STARS and trips to DISNEYLAND.

At the moment ALEX is playing his taped music, BIRDS FLY OVER THE RAINBOW OH WHY OH WHY CAN'T I?

And would you believe it, NO REQUEST IS TOO EXTREME WHEN YOU WISH UPON A STAR AS DREAMERS DO Followed up with AT LAST IS `BETHLEHEM' IN SIGHT FOR THE LITTLE DONKEY? and will her dreams that the manuscript will be accepted, come true—

The great day came when the letter arrived to say that the publisher was interested in the manuscript sample and wanted to see more.

At six o'clock the next morning, I turned the bedside lamp on, scarcely daring to believe it could be true and read the letter again. The lamp was standing against a little bevelled mirror, the reflection must have caused a prism (is that the right word, I wonder?), and stretching right across the page was a RAINBOW.

I knew then that the book would be accepted, as if I was going to be disappointed, there is no way the DP's would have let me hold the letter in that position. When the manuscript was posted I remembered a story, I should have included so decided to take it.

On the day that I had arranged to take the manuscript to London, ordered a taxi to take me to the bus. Our taxi service is run by such kind people and I have never known them to be anything else but strictly on time. I don't know how they do it, but that morning PETER turned up too early. I had fifteen minutes to wait. I didn't mind, of course, but was surprised as he had never done that before. Actually, he probably was a bit surprised himself but if he ever gets to read this, he will have the explanation.

As I waited for the bus a beautiful RAINBOW formed. It was a perfect bow complete from end to end. Had PETER been on time, I would have missed it.

When I arrived in London, I found helpful people all the way. I was handed a map and noticed the name of the area where my father had lived and with his famous tutor VAN BRINE, had studied his cello.

I recalled the recent offering of EASTENDERS where MINTY was looking at an old film called THE BROKEN MELODY. The title of the musical theatre production that made VAN BEINE famous. I had said to ALEX, "What on earth is he doing in EASTENDERS, our story is going back to 1915 for heaven's sake," so we laughed, as you can imagine.

The film was repeated in the telly play THE LAND GIRLS in which there was a Cockney girl called Connie.

I was wondering why the film was shown twice, but now realise that the title of the film was sad so they had to show it twice, so that the negative could be reversed. When I wrote to the BBC to ask where they got it from, they so kindly said `AMAZON´, are we into' TROPICAL PLANTS again? I thought.

Their reply had for its logo that little map that they show at the beginning of their programme, and I thought of Uncle George's OLD FATHER THAMES song.

I looked at the map that I had been handed in London when it dawned on me, no wonder they had kept on about RUBBER TREES, SPITFIRES, KEYS and GREENHOUSES!

The publishers whose destiny it is to bring this *Important* story to the world is in the DOCK area and must be within the sound of Aunt Daisies' LONDON BELLS. I knew then that CONNIE'S SAILING SHIP had indeed come into harbour.

The stories went on coining in - SNOW WHITE, JACK'S BEANSTALK, ALADDIN, BOY BLUE, A LITTLE DOG LAUGHED TO SEE SUCH FUN, CINDERELLA AND

A POLICEMAN'S BALL and many more.

We have a stunning friend, so kind, nothing is too much trouble for him. He has a habit lately of turning up suddenly when help is needed and seems to appear from nowhere as he did on the day of the SEAGULLS. Totally unaware of how attractive he is, ALAN too was once in a vicious circle. Just as simply, his problem was explained as was GLEN'S. He `walks tall' now and has gone on to make his life a success.

What Supermen they have had to be to recover and remain the lovely people they are in spite of all they have been through.

I can see from my window the POSTBOX - children are playing by it in big groups these days. They have a YO-YO craze again and are part of the Dimension kids' efforts to tell me that a letter from the publisher will be coming soon. They used a story too of POSTMAN PAT AND HIS MISSING BLACK AND WHITE CAT who came in out of the fog, to tell me.

When I was at last able to discuss it with her SHEILA had said, having written books of her own, "It's an ever-continuing story, how can you end it?"

As I write ALEX is playing a song chat was the opening number to a show that ALAN stage managed for us.

LET THE PEOPLE SING I know SUPERMAN that's it, SUPERMAN, he'll do.

Until now, never in the whole of mankind's history have we been able to know exactly what happens when this section of life ends. But for people in history who were willing to suffer for our sake we wouldn't have been in time to save it all. We still haven't got the whole explanation of how the power works that keeps us going, but you can bet your life they'll think of some way to tell us all we need to know.

JILL is an expert in astrology. I call her STAR as she is one and no mistake. Other young people came out into the light besides ALAN, each time understanding the misery theory and their heredity. I was not wholly in accord with JILL that ASTROLOGY would be an important part of our future, but as time went on, I was forced to change my ideas as so many of her personality assessments became more and more accurate.

Outside her house one night with my little grandson (the one in the POPPY story), when he exclaimed, "COR! LOOK AT ALL THOSE STARS NAN, THERE'S MILLIONS." I replied, "YES DARLING," and thought HOW CAN THEY NOT BE PART OF US IN SOME WAY?

As the new knowledge comes, gradually at first, then the CHAIN REACTION OF JOY WILL SPIN EVERYWHERE AROUND THE WORLD, WITH TOTAL PEACE OE MIND, THERE WILL BE NO PROBLEM THAT MANKIND CANNOT SOLVE TO SURVIVE BECAUSE HE WILL BE SUPERMAN

Epilogue

One fine day in June, the MIDSUMMER sun was shining when the post arrived with the manuscript after my proofreading for my final check. It was still months before it was complete and I never did overcome the typing, but the day dawned when the last page was put in. Feeling the strain, I decided to catch a bus, a long long, journey somewhere new would be the answer.

On the way we stopped at a village displaying a poster for a "FESTIVAL 'OF BELLS". As the buses run through there every hour I alighted, thinking that there would be just enough time.

The church was made beautiful with floral displays depicting all the London churches that are mentioned in the nursery rhyme ORANGES AND LEMONS to celebrate the refurbishment of the bells that after many years now ring out merrily.

Then I remembered the date, it was BRIGADOON DAY.

The backlog manifested itself some weeks later. It must have been a subconscious worry over a long period that it wouldn't be accepted as the generated misery (negative) must then be burnt out. The symptoms lasted several days so I checked them out with my doctor who reassured me, and from then on I made a rapid recovery'.

Just as I had finished this, the sun was rising, I looked up from my work and the perfect oblong of light was on the PICTURE for the second time. The words of the HOLY CITY came to mind.

SING FOR THE NIGHT IS O'ER

As time went on hints did seem to come in that could explain a little about how the power works.

In one of JILL'S new age books I read of KIRLIAN PHOTOGRAPHY. This apparently is a camera that can photograph an AURA that surrounds people and I believe all living things. It is like a glow that becomes strong when we are happy and less so when we are miserable. This must be the power that we generate when a lot of people are together in a JOY situation. It may be the explanation for why we are suddenly healed at a religious gathering sometimes, and where the strength comes to complete lengthy FUN RUNS. When one thinks of how many finish the course it is remarkable. Many people who have taken part have talked of a MAGICAL ATMOSPHERE during the London Marathon. So, if there is anything in this then the opposite must apply and so concentrating on negative things, (which is difficult to avoid when our joy level is low), we are likely to be more sensitive to aches and pains.

If we can get into a crowd of happy people enjoying the same things that we do, it is highly possible that we will feel better. I can see why we haven't been able to fully take advantage of this healing simplicity as the backlog will come on sooner or later, either after a prolonged spell of loneliness, or if physical pain is relieved, as it can be when we come into this healing power that comes with large groups of happy people. Sometimes we can wake up feeling worse than we did before, not realising that it is only TEMPORARY. During this time, we can't hear the subconscious healing voice of our loved ones in the

Dimension, like we've switched off our radios, although they can transmit comfort through other people around us. We only have to wait for the battery charge to burn out which it will and the improvement that we have gained from our experience of a JOY generating situation will return.

Once we understand what is happening to us the period of backlog will be uncomfortable but harmless because we won't recharge it with fear. When our JOY level is at its highest point the Dimension people can make themselves heard by our subconscious mind and give us inner peace. Without subconscious worry our body can get on with the business of correcting itself.

They are getting their work force built up now and so we may very well hear of more people who eventually feel better once the effects of the backlog can be fully understood.

We know that this isn't the whole story of the power but DORIS spoke of EARTH ENERGIES. I don't know much about these but before a sequel to this is begun (whoever writes it, may not be myself), I hope a lot more information that can connect the AURA with how our personalities earn" on as they obviously do, will be available.

Also, I hope that they will be able to explain how it is that some people have been able to be aware of the Dimension people even when they have great distress. The ANGEL OF MONS that is talked about in the First World War when a lot of soldiers saw the figure in the sky comforting them is an example. Their misery level must have been full up to the brim but there would have been a lot of soldiers in the Dimension by then to stand SHOULDER TO SHOULDER to convey the compassionate power to overcome it.

I wonder if modern day awareness in times of distress could be influenced by our tranquillising medication too? If we just hold on, I am sure they will give us ALL the answers eventually.

When the understanding does come of how the power works, which it will, I don't see any reason, just like in the fairy tales of old, why the world shouldn't live HAPPILY EVER AFTER

ACKNOWLEDGEMENTS

I give my grateful thanks to the L R Price editors for their courage in launching such an unusual project and for their COMPASSION so that we can replace our tears with a **SONG IN OUR HEARTS**

"THERE'S A RAINBOW ON THE RIVER" was written some time ago. It is a mere fraction of the information which has come in since it was published by Austin and Macauley some years ago. There Is no doubt that the comfort and peace of mind that the world has never known until now is on its way, ... rather like the moment just before dawn when there is a glow along the horizon heralding a sunny day. Thanks to such brave people as Sally Morgan and Teresa Cuputo - who with others who can pick up the language of the Dimension people and are filling theatres and television programmes all over. Brave because this is the most difficult thing to get to the world as up until now the "Backlog trauma" will often affect everyone who has been subconsciously unaware of the presence of our loved ones who have gone before us, *so* after a short while, will go into REVERSE and reject it. This combined with the fact that when our misery levels are at their highest during times of grief and made worse when we are in a group of grieving people, the barrier between us and our loved ones becomes stronger and when we most need their comfort it is difficult for them to make us aware of it.

Now that SALLY and people like her have been broadcasting for such a long time, people are gradually getting used to this traumatic change and the 'backlog' reaction is becoming less frequent. The right timing for 'THERE'S A RAINBOW ON THE RIVER' is not far away I am sure. However long it takes, all WILL become clear in the end. THE EXPLANATION FOR THE REVERSE REACTION IS IN THE book. This COULD BE THE MOST IMPORTANT INFORMATION THAT IT CONVEYS TO US. This ceases to be a problem once we understand how it works.

The invisible language did not end with the completion of THERE'S A RAINBOW ON THE RIVER" but continued bringing more and more information to further our understanding of why this has not reached humanity until now on any big scale, with it the explanation for why Austin Macauley could no longer publish it.

Sooner or later people are going to start being more positive when the backlog trauma (Which is what this reverse behaviour is} burns out. My brother worked all over the world. When he visited me and was suffering from backlog, - (In the book) he drove on the wrong side of the road!

"DP's' had made sure nothing was coming the other

way as they would have been aware or his vulnerability. When SALLY and people like her address an audience they do. They have to have a lot of `DPS' to look out for people who may be vulnerable so as to see them home safely. This is one of the reasons for building up their workforce before this book comes on the market. This is the reason for keeping sales of THERE'S A RAINBOW ON THE RIVER back until the right timing, only they know when that is.

In the dimension, the number of people has increased to share the workload because filled with hope that the end of this separation from their loved ones can be brought to an end, their own misery levels are towering and their positive power is stronger. Enthusiasm is generating Joy still further, so they reassure us that no matter how long it takes, sooner or later, in the end, ALL WILL BE WELL.

Hence my attention is so frequently drawn to advertisements to sow wild flower seeds to encourage BUSY BEES, BUZBY BARKLEY, (associated with FRED ASTAIRES films), they called him BUZZ, and BUZZ ALDRIN. Wasn't he the first man on the moon? No, one of the space team anyway, (too many references to write them all down although I have had a try) and to ALL HANDS ON DECK*

The following narrative is an example of the way they put information across. I am not very good at learning computer skills, having had no training, just had to press all the keys to try to find out what they do. So, when I wrote to the publishers, I remarked "If you needed to learn to sing, I would be on home ground and know what I was doing". _ and referred to the song `I'D LIKE TO TEACH THE WORLD TO SING IN PERFECT HARMONY' but had paraphrased the words to WE'RE GOING TO TEACH THE

WORLD TO SING IN PERFECT HARMONY.

I had recorded a programme at Christmas. It was the SINGING IN THE WORKPLACE finals to be performed in ELY Cathedral. The performance was created by the amazing GARETH MALONE. Among the finalists were BANKING and based in Canary Wharf where the publishers of THERE'S A RAINBOW ON THE RIVER have their office. I was astonished to see what looked like a shot of the reception area where I had tried to leave the revolving door too soon and bumped my head against the glass. What will the Dimension people think of next! But they will be very close to Gareth. Do you know that he started out alone armed only with someone with a camera, a portable piano and determination (I think it was Birmingham) and asked people in the street doing their shopping if they would like to form a choir! Can you imagine anything more challenging? The things he has got people to achieve since takes our breath away. If a reader has read THERE'S A RAINBOW ON THE RIVER then they will understand the power of the RUBBER TREE PLANT which Gareth is an example, of how one person can give positive JOY to the world and the POSITIVE POWER that can come with it.

The Dimension people can give us the ideas but we have to do the work so I wonder how many hours Gareth had to strive to achieve such musical genius.

Programmes referring to people trying to go through glass doors including an advert (I think it was broadband?) and two funny BEES one of which bumps into glass an advertisement that went on and on about two funny BEES and they were trying to get into an office (I think it was Broadband or something anyway, one of them tries to get through glass mistaking it for a door and bumps himself (which seemed familiar.) As with a lot of this repetition the DP's are trying to tell us something important. And I know now what that must have been.

The point that they are making is "It is TOO SOON" the timing must be right. Austin Macauley were just its custodians.

After the book was complete, I tried to keep a record of events that followed. They are many pages of transcript and even then, it would be impossible to record everything. It does look as if a sequel may be in the future plans at some time or other. To try to include it all now would, I think overload you.

It may be important to include just a rough synopsis of a few pages, but they are only a tiny bit of the information that is being told us. I can only include here a mere scrap but the point that is being made is the dimensions efforts to tell us at what point they have reached in the battle to overcome the obstacles that they have to surmount, likening its progress to the World War 2.

My Dear ALEX joined them last year. Like me he had become used to the language that was projected to us. When a friend lost his little Doggie called FRED, advertisements came up on the telly about a doggie called FRED and other references that couldn't be mistaken as they were so frequent. By that time, he and I had learned laughter which we couldn't share with our friend or anyone. It was such a shame but for the time being this had to be borne as there was nothing we could do about it.

His remark when Fred's identity came up was "Well, I be B…..rd! clever stuff isn't it. The story of how ALEX got his identity across when he joined them was amazing.

People around me couldn't understand my lack of grief. I have tried to record some of it. The emphasis on his D DAY experiences uppermost.

Last week I saw staring up at me, outside a charity shop, a book 'THE PEGASUS BRIDGE'. Its cover a photo of the soldiers as they are leaving their glider. As ALEX has now drawn attention to this time often, as he was among this brave bunch of young men, I thought it was one of the times that he just checks in and checks out again as he often does. He can't stay with me long because they have vital work to do and they take turns to look after us, as it would be very boring if they had to stay with one person all the time really, no matter how much they love us, but they make sure that someone is. The next day on the Yesterdays programme was a film of the actual landing exactly like the one on the book cover, the following events that the film portrayed were traumatic. They know I am anxious about what I am going to include in this letter to you so they must be directing me. For which I am truly grateful as it is a responsibility and it alarms me sometimes and worry generates misery and so I could become incompetent, so they try to make me understand that I must trust them as, they are in the driving seat.

In his identity check in, when he went into the dimension, ALEX used Greek Mythology. It is all too long to include now but they went on about the PHOENIX. In the mythological tales, this is a bird that rises from the ashes.

"There must be a reason for its frequency, they've given me quite complicated puzzles to solve before this"

When peace of mind that comes with the awareness of the dimension, Scientists and Heads of State and others who have the security of whole countries in their hands will be able to make more positive decisions and positive power will grow. (This will take time of course, slowly at first but it will grow and one day before long, others will start to notice a positive tendency. A bit like the dawn in the morning before the sun is beginning to come up. Had the multi heritage been left to evolve on its own it would have been too late to solve the climate problem. They have to somehow get us through this era of transition when we are beginning to realise that our consciousness is permanent.

To demonstrate how determined the dimension people have to be, they saw to it that I would see a film called THE FLIGHT OF THE PHOENIX. with JAMES STEWART, a story of a plane crew who crashed in the desert and they had to have the most amazing determination and ingenuity to survive. When ALEX and I went to the area on the Norfolk and Suffolk borders where I had lived as a child near an American Airbase. The Flying Fortresses as I believe the B17 s were called used to come back in the evening returning from raids on Germany, and one day one was just over my head just hanging in there with its engines clattering and rattling. There was no explosion so it must have got down OK. We learned when we went to DISS on a visit, that JAMES STEWART the film star was based there and in a pub is a photo of him in his plane. When the film was advertised and I saw it once more on the telly, my son came in and said "Saw a good film last night, THE MEMPHIS BELLE", a true story of *a* plane crews' last mission; a B17 I believe. So, it reminded me of the morning when the plane was so crippled when I was there. I remembered that whenever I was exposed to danger, circumstances would move me to safety as within a short time we were living in a remote part of the Pennines where it was safe. I was typing this and to relax I put the telly on and the programme was showing a film of 1943, the summer I was there and saw the plane. JAMES STEWART was giving an interview, in his uniform, his face drawn and tired. I thought it so kind of him to take time off to speak to the film crew. On the actual day of JAMES STEWART's Yesterday film, I went to straighten a photo of ALEX in his uniform that was Hanging a bit lopsided on the wall, only to notice for the first time the date, it was taken in 1943 Indicating still further that they want us to notice the date and time lapse, with many other references to 1943.

Shortly after, I had typed this, the song COMING IN ON A WING AND A PRAYER

The Dimension people have an enormous challenge equal to the organising of D Day, when it took the combined ideas of the most experienced people in the world to work out the tactics to defeat the biggest threat to mankind that has ever been known. Because the selective breeding that the enemy had in mind would have delayed the evolving of the more developed mind and we would not have been in time to be able to pick up the guidance of an intelligence far ahead of our own as it will be when the world is aware everywhere of the presence of this wonderful, never been known on any big scale before, comfort, so reducing our misery and making us more receptive to positive guidance.

The big problem that they face is the effect of the backlog reaction. As we know from history how so many people suffered because of their insight as in Jesus, and the Christians who followed him ending up in a Lion's den as they did. Joan of Arc and the psychic people who were persecuted as they were and condemned as witches. Even in recent days, Air Chief Marshall Lord Hugh Dowding, the architect of THE BATTLE OF BRITAIN, who could see the Pilots after they had been shot down, confused and not knowing what had happened. He would give them reassurance that someone would find them and explain. There were so many people going at the same time it is highly possible that there weren't enough positive dimension people to get to them all at once to explain to them what had happened. The misery would have affected some of them in the dimension too, just as it does us, so that this would stop their ability to be able to help because we can't function in a positive way when our negative battery charge is high. There must have been a large positive group by then though otherwise we wouldn't have won. All thanks to people in history who suffered for mankind's sake so as to get this vital knowledge to us. The enormous problem the DP's have to overcome is the fact that when we have any worry or fears resolved, after a time has elapsed, its length varying on the extent of our worry, we suffer from a post traumatic period that is only TEMPORARY. If we understand it we will not recharge the battery by being alarmed. During this time, we will have a tendency to go into REVERSE. Psychiatrists are coming up with this theory too that Jesus stopped people's fears and so they went IN REVERSE and by the time they were in crowds, as in the coliseum in ROME where the Christians were sent, the negative would have charged at a faster rate.

It has been acknowledged that the architect of THE BATTLE OF BRITAIN was AIR CHIEF MARSHALL LORD DOWDING, and that his guidance was correct. He was sent to America and never heard THE BELLS of London that were rung to celebrate the end of this momentous battle. Had we lost it the outlook does not bear thinking about and so much we owe to him (and others of course). It was half a century before a memorial was erected to Lord Dowding, I think it is ST. CLEMENTS Church in London. There were other reasons for why he was treated in this way I believe, but to my eyes, it does follow the pattern.

At this time, I had found an old newspaper. I didn't read it at the time and had meant to give it to my son but had forgotten and it stayed beneath my piano lid until many months after when I came across it again. To my astonishment, its date, June 6th 1944 told of the first D Day landings. It must have been a very early edition to be published so soon. ALEX's group were out there several hours before the Armada that they could see beneath them from their glider. And the fact that my attention wasn't drawn to it till many months after their frequent references to 1943 relevant.

In the notes is a colourful story about COVER GIRL, the film that I had seen when I had the presentiment that I would one day be involved in show business.

In the newspaper was an advertisement and write up of the film COVER GIRL and a reference to the lovely lively rendering of **A NEW DAY TOMORROW**.

I had been wondering if that would make a good title for a sequel in due course. In the D DAY film, the words of a Glider Pilot, who had been in the same action as ALEX and the PEGASUS BRIDGE, "There will be a NEW TOMORROW". So they were trying to instruct me in some way with the D DAY NEWSPAPER.

They want us to understand the point at which they have reached in their fight to get the positive upper hand in

207

our affairs and in the same way they have reached the equivalent of D DAY, so it may not be too long before they are on the "Home run" towards our NEW TOMORROW.

 LETS KEEP ON SINGING MAKE

WAY FOR TOMORROW THE SUN IS BRINGING A NEW

DAY TOMORROW

The Dimension people use Fairy Tales for instance. When they want to attract my attention to a particular member of my family or friends, they will remind me of a favourite Fairy-tale which has significance to what they want to convey. They have been doing this for years. I am sure children are involved, even the high possibility that they are behind a lot of the ideas too. The following ones an example.

RED RIDING HOOD — My daughter and her family. When the Dimension people want to tell me about them as she fives away? TWO people get on the bus or the street wearing red jackets with a hood. Or references to RED RIDING HOOD on the telly or in books. When they want me to distinguish which one of her family they are alluding to, something will turn up associated with one of them like a remark about CASABLANCA (as BEN my daughters husband did in the story in THERE'S A RAINBOW ON THE RIVER) Or if the repeated RED JACKETS turn up at the same time as a big blacks shaggy dog then it will be my daughter that they are referring to as she looked after Danny for a time and adored him. (In the book). Sure enough there would be an email from one of them or something.

ALICE IN WONDERLAND is referring to my son's family. Songs and references to that story. (repeatedly) then there is always a reason. For another friend CHITTY CHITTY BANG BANG. Fortunately, she has caught on and follows the guidance, which for me is a great stride. They have names for us all too. The young lady who does this is called TRULY Scrumptious from CHITTY CHITTY BANG BANG. She makes the most amazing cakes and fits the bill.

My grandson has no problem either. As a little boy he was puzzled that others weren't aware of the same thing, but then he has a mute heritage background as long as your arm (as the saying goes.)

Another friend is called a **BLUEBIRD** because of her natural ability to cheer people up with her delightful wit. When she is around, depression disappears like magic. With so many people now it would be impossible to write them all down. I am known as `CINDERELLA' and the story of how that came about is quite along one but I have been assured that although now l am elderly the name still applies! Alex's sister, **THE SLEEPING BEAUTY,** as she played the part of Fairy fortitude in our own production and was born ST GEORGES DAY (and the DRAGON)and it was in the Disney version the clue as to why the book wouldn't self. It was many months before I realised that this was serious. Austin Macauley were concerned, (I tried to explain to them the reason but by that time so many of the staff had changed and it is highly possible that no one was left who had actually read the book, as they are producing new ones all the time.

So, they can be forgiven for not understanding what I was talking about when I assured them that there was no cause for alarm. I will enclose an account of what inspired me to come to that conclusion in time.

So many Fairy tales and Nursery rhymes they have touched on it would be impossible to record them all. My Doctor friend **PINOCHIO** and his lovely wife who is a Methodist lay preacher is **THE BLUE FAIRY. CAMELOT** was a real lark. My brother who is with them now uses **A THOUSAND AND ONE NIGHTS** and in `COVER GIRL' a young man with such a familiar smile among other hints says **"CLIMB ABOARD MY MAGIC CARPET AND AWAY WE'LL GO"**

When the war ended, I lived with my mother in the North country. We had a little bungalow in the hills that was twenty-five minutes' walk from the village where it was necessary to catch a tram into Blackburn, where in a dress shop I worked as a sixteen year old Junior which was just another name for a general `Dogsbody' at everyone's beck and call, although I was extraordinarily happy. (I was reminded of this by the video of HALF A SIXPENCE, the story of KIPPS, who was a Drapers assistant in a shop like the one I worked in). One day the seamstresses were calling me from upstairs and a sales lady was calling from the sales floor. Half way up the stairs at the time, unsure of who to answer first and customers laughing, like the song In Wait Disney's CINDERELLA, which goes

CINDERELLA CINDERELLA ALL I HEAR
IS CINDERELLA FROM THE MOMENT THAT I WAKE
UP ITS CALLING CALLING CALLING ....

Sung by the mice. They had a little mouse too, (Gosh
I had forgotten that till now.)

In the 1947 winter, the snowdrifts were nine-foot-tall
until spring. Extreme weather is not entirely new as anyone
who was in the North at that time will tell you. When I got
home, water had to be got from the farm as we had no taps
in those days. My brother was still in the regular Navy. We
were happy enough though then, to have somewhere safe
to live in those days.

One day a **POLICEMAN'S** ball was on everyone's
mind, austerity was still with us and I think so was clothing
coupons (I must check that). There was a lovely market
though (still is) and my mother had spotted some crushed-
up material in a box. When she got it home and it was
ironed, it turned out to be the most stunning shot taffeta. It
shone and when it caught the light would change from
silvery white into palest blue and back again,

I haven't seen anything quite like it since except in
the Welt Disney version of **CINDERELLA**. The North was
the home of textile manufacturing and my mother thought
that it was a new experimental material that had been
discarded. I had made up my mind that I would make up
the dress as I was conscious of the fact that my mother
waited on me hand and foot so we found in a Magazine, a
picture of a gown fit for a princess, with little cap sleeves. It
had gloves but these were unobtainable. We decided the

hair would have to go up in the same way.

The day came for me to get on with it but I was too tired and the date of the ball was coming near. I had to hurry home to be in time for "**DICK BARTON SPECIAL AGENT**" on the radio at a quarter to seven in the evening so thinking about it now, how far it was from the village, it's not surprising that I couldn't get on with the dress.

Our little bungalow had to have its walls decorated. We couldn't get wallpaper so many of us had to try to think of other ways to brighten our homes and one of them was to stipple. Emulsion paint wasn't around then, we had to use something called distemper a kind of water paint. It was hard work and only a clever person could make this satisfactory. My mother had the idea to use a little piece of crunched up cloth and dip it in coloured paint and stipple a design like a bowed three-piece screen. It was quite pretty really considering that decorating a house was not her in natural comfort zone, but she would always have a warm fire and a lovely meal ready when I got home. (I wonder now how she did that, I must have brought the groceries as there were no shops anywhere near). The time drew near but the dress wasn't even started.

One evening I came in to the living room and there on the wall hanging right in the centre of the screen like design was the loveliest dress anyone could have seen. The dresses were so important to everyone at the shop after so much austerity and we hardly talked of anything else. It was going to be a challenge to make a Cinderella out of me but the dress would have made a Cinderella out of anybody. Being the most junior and the most inferior member of the staff I was looking forward to arriving and surprising everyone in my shimmering pale blue and silver

A RAINBOW ON THE RIVER

white creation, after all they didn't know that my mother had trained in a top drawer store in London (TOP SHOP now) and later running her own business was an artist of the first degree. I had no partner to take me but knew that my colleagues from the shop would be there and I was looking forward to my entry.

But it was not to be, I never got to that POLICEMAN'S BALL. The weather turned nasty. It was unbelievable just how terrible the English weather can be. There was no way to get there through so much gale, rain and mud. Taxis were unheard of then so far out in the country. I was broken hearted but my mother could always think of an answer (I will never forget her words) 'life will not always be disappointing like this Darling. Your turn **WILL** come and (Metaphorically speaking) "**ONE DAY YOU WILL GET TO THE BALL**".

Her words were indelible in my memory and were fulfilled just as she had predicted. Many years later ALEX worked on a farm and we had a tied cottage in a village miles away from anywhere. I never lost sight of how fortunate we were to live in such beautiful countryside with our happy healthy children, but it was so dull. All the same we still managed to walk miles to get a bus to go into the little town to see the Walt Disney films. (Little did I suspect what an important part that cinema was to play for all of us) together with ALEX's sister who was even more isolated than myself. It was then I noticed how some of the characters would remind me of someone, for instance, MRS JUMBO (DUMBO) so like a wonderful grandmother we knew and ALEX's sister had the lovely long hair and sweet nature of AURORA in THE SLEEPING BEAUTY. She later played the part of FAIRY FORTITUDE in our production (aptly named) and sang so beautifully OVER THE RAINBOW. She is in the dimension now and not surprising that all references to that show is likely to have some importance in some direction.

When I was reunited after many years with ROSE (The BLUE ROSE STORY) she remarked that when they saw the film of CINDERELLA were reminded of myself. I couldn't see any resemblance as she is beautiful although I had the same colour hair and hairstyle, even the little costume was familiar. I was given some collectors plates of scenes from the film too, the subject attracting my attention which of course it was meant to do.

The plates have the scene where the mice opened the screen to reveal the lovely dress, it was shortly after that I remembered the day when I was surprised, as Cinderella was, to see the dress hanging in the middle of a screen: She too had been kept busy and so didn't have time to make the dress in time so her MICE friends had made it while she was not there. Also, she didn't get to the ball in that dress. The baddy sisters tore it from her and so she ran into the garden in despair. As she runs out into the garden it was then it struck a familiar chord. Her FAIRY GODMOTHER came to the rescue as we all know. And she was provided with the shimmering white gown to catch the light as mine did turning it in to the palest shimmering blue as material that is 'shot' will do.

To relieve the boredom when our children grew older, I had the inspiration to produce a show in the village hall. This was very difficult as television had not been in for long and no one wanted to go out in the evenings. But I felt desperate need keep struggling to get it off the ground. It became imperative that I pulled it off, no matter how

challenging but knew not why. I was joined in time by
lovely talented people who supported me and so together
we presented a huge success with our JACK AND THE
BEAN STALK and After FIVE riotous productions, we had
to leave the village and move into the town.

From the very first week I was to find a welcome
that, when I look back now, was far above the average.
Someone in almost every house in the long street became
interested and were to support me along with people in the
town in my rather ambitious plans. They had a wonderful
Carnival club too, and one year they created five floats from
this one street.

For this I was an onlooker as I was busy with the
shows for the Cinema. Even the young Cinema manager
lived a few doors away. With an army of volunteers to
complete the miracle and an unusually above average talent
of my loving friends we danced and sang our way through
many years of full-scale productions.

As the years went on, I began to notice the
coincidences They were so frequent that it would be
impossible to record them all.

For instance, a chappie who was so funny, like so
many of them his performance was positively professional.
When he traced his ancestry was flabbergasted to see that
he was descended from WEE GEORGIE WOOD, a famous
old MUSIC HALL star. My mother had often talked about
him. When in the ROYAL NAVY he had been stationed at
the same shore based NAVAL STATION as at one time
Row had. When he went into the Dimension, instead of
using one of his songs or something like that, he used
references to his NAVAL Service, that was unmistakably his
identity. It's a pity I can't write up the details but it would

take too much space. So, the suspicion I have had that the two instances are linked could be true. The high standard of talent the people who I now realise were ordained to be involved could be no accident.

TWO talented young men who unbeknown to each other worked for the same AERONAUTICAL FACTORY miles away made the decision to come here to live simultaneously. It was the same factory that PAUL in the faggot story had done training as an AERONAUTICAL ENGINEER.

As the manager had to keep Bingos and FILMS going as long as possible, we could not take the scenery and costumes into the cinema until a couple of days before our dress rehearsal and our first of six nights performances. I had to play the piano for rehearsals but the cast made no secret of their relief when dedicated musicians came on the end to give us their experienced musical backing. The way the chorus ladies and chaps dealt with so many costume changes in the short time they had and the efficiency of the volunteer back stage team with the ten children, would fill a professional artist with admiration. I used to paint the scenery. We had six scenes in THE SLEEPING BEAUTY, and in that short time our dedicated stage managers used to assemble and hang it. And with the lighting expertise of our experienced Carnival Crew and the cooperation of our young Manager, against all odds, the curtain always went up on time. We did twelve full scale shows and some little ones the people in the village were just as capable and talented, it became obvious after a time that something was guiding me as I never had any problem with thinking up the designs as they were always there in my mind. I had thought of it in a spiritual sense. Though it wasn't until the

BRIGADOON experience that I realised with shock that it was all done by PEOPLE! The word SPIRIT seems inappropriate somehow now as anything less like SPIRITS I can't imagine as they so strong.

It was during this time that I noticed the connection between the GENERATING JOY in CROWDS and its healing influence.

At the last count we had fifty-five on stage and altogether an eighty strong company A television presenter became interested and arranged to come with cameras to make a little programme about us but the Cinema had to be sold and we had to stop.

It was I realise now the training ground for the writing of THERE'S A RAINBOW ON THE RIVER.

My Mothers foresight did indeed turn out to be accurate as did my own presentiment that I mention in THERE'S A RAINBOW ON RIVER, that I would one day be part of this entertainment so important to the world. The story of how this came about is too long now as this is just a synopsis to explain how the invisible language progressed but it would have to be included if a sequel was written.

I was at least thirty years old before the destiny materialised to produce musical shows and Panto and so with enthusiastic friends we danced and sang our way through fourteen productions.

I have not quite given up hope that one day I may do one more show although I am elderly now there is a first time for everything and age is not going to take its toll in the way that it has with previous generations when a peace of mind comes that has never been experienced before in the history of mankind. This has to be very slow though but already a hundred years old is becoming the norm here. But the Dimension people may have other work for me, as they will for many others in this fight to get this knowledge to everyone. It is a fight, but they have assured me that more and more people are joining them because this has to have dedication and hard work just as it does on this side of the `gauze".

The DP's have explained why it is that people associate them with ethereal beings and angels and sometimes other worldliness. This is essential for the time being sometimes, because to realise that they are people just the same as we are and part of the same world the shock is too much to handle and like Pit ponies who work in the dark can't take the sun and have to be blinkered and so we turn away from it. But we become higher in intelligence when in the dimension, far higher than when we are although they say that we will catch up to them one day.

And so my mother's prediction did literally come true when we did a show which was a cavalcade of laughter and song, I did not have to go on stage much after but in that first show I sang a song called "WALKING IN THE CLOUDS" dressed in a white crinoline like something from "GONE WITH THE WIND" and singing happily the second verse I was joined from out of the wings by a beautiful) young man in his scarlet jacket, laden with epaulets and gold braid who waltzed me round and round To the audiences applause. Because so many of them knew him, he was the local POLICEMAN, so I did get to the" ball after all ...

A THEATRICAL GAUZE is a transparent curtain on which a scene is painted. When a light is directed on it the scene looks solid but when the light is turned off and is then shown on a stage behind it the front picture disappears and the scene behind it lights up it seems to me a good description of our view of the Dimension which up to now has been invisible.

This was just the beginning, as the years went on more and more, I was in time trained to recognise the reason for and the meaning behind so many of the references to these subjects and to translate what I am being told, and when I did catch on to what they are meaning I would get a KITE! They never fail to see to it that I would see a KITE or sometimes an old flying machine of long ago (often called a KITE). So it was that I did not get alarmed when the book simply wouldn't sell. I tried to explain to the publishers that there was no cause for alarm. To explain this to me the dimension people called my attention to the video of THE SLEEPING BEAUTY. The point is made when the Prince is trapped on a mountain by a fear some dragon only the SWORD OF TRUTH is left for him to survive to rescue AURORA (translated THE DAWN) the TIMING is vital dangerously near the edge of the cliff he must throw the SWORD OF TRUTH at exactly the right moment. One moment too soon or too late and all would be lost. His TIMING is correct and he hurls it right into the heart of the dragon destroying misery for ever (The misery of our unawareness of our loved ones).

I am confident that sales of THERE'S A RAINBOW ON THE RIVER are not far away, all thanks to people like Sally and TERESA who are gradually bringing this revelation to the world and bravely facing the opposition that the backlog causes for some.

It was 1947 when the dress was made so I think the designs for the CINDERELLA film were made by then. It says on the video that it won Best musical! score of 1950. My

219

mother had not seen it and it was twenty years later before I did. I was wondering if the Dimension people thought up the idea before it was made or after. There is a high possibility that the film came first and the idea afterwards. It was years and years before that they started to think up the code idea, as so many of the films they use are very old. They don't work what we would call miracles. Everything they have influenced so far has had an understandable explanation. Scientists are coming up with a theory of a time thing, and many people on YouTube have had experience of previous lives. They can't all be wrong I am sure that there is something in this but our group in the Dimension have chosen to only use a system that we can understand for the moment. But you can bet your life sooner or later they will educate us all as the multi heritage becomes more normal to understand all that they do... There is a strong possibility that children, in their desperation to make their parents understand, would have been persuaded they could help by looking for ideas to get this message over to us, and they may well have spotted the material that was so like Cinderella's dress in the film. Sooner or later they will tell us if I have got it right (Perhaps I will get a kite!) It would be feasible that kids are coming up with ideas as so many are based on children's stuff and it must help to lower their misery level which works the same as it does for us. They have made it clear that they take turns in watching me to keep me safe, (WE'RE ON THE BEAT as the Policeman's song goes. In THERE'S A RAINBOW ON THE RIVER")

This certainly has been thought of long long ago, Sylvia, my little dancing friend used to appear all over England and Ireland with her dancing act. I hadn't met her till she had retired and had joined our company to teach our lovely chorus girls. (We had boys as well) As my mother and I had lived in many places Sylvia and I realised with astonishment that we had been following each other around. When we were in Norfolk she was in NORWICH and the Grand theatre in BLACKBURN at the time I was there and again in TAUNTON. At the time of the dress shop, the following summer we spent a week in FLEETWOOD and the only thing I can remember about it except for a ferry which was to prove relevant later on as well, was a performance of a sister act in the theatre Follies, Sylvia had performed in many many seaside variety shows and does not remember the date she was there, neither do I except that it was the summer after that awful winter in 1947, but knowing what I do now the possibility that the sister act was hers is high, and our meeting was no accident. (they were called the Arllete Sisters).

Sylvia is in the dimension now and she uses SNOW WHITE AND THE SEVEN DWARFS. This came about because she had a tiny figure with thick shiny black hair worn in a wavy bob. With a tiny cottage, donkeys' years old, someone had made for her kitchen a tiny table and seats to match made from wood with a design of red flowers. One day she had washed her hair and tied around it a band with a little bow in the front, standing in the doorway of her kitchen with the sun behind her, she could have played SNOW WHITE on stage and got away with it, even at her age. The point that she has made is sooner or later everyone everywhere will have a HAPPY ENDING ......

An up to date example of now they give advice. I have a round cushion which had turned up at a jumble sale.

On it an appliqué not quite life-size, but noticeable, face of CINDERELLA in her shimmering blue dress, hair up as I had mine for some years. She is smiling out at us.

The last few days this APRIL, strong sunshine has been with us for a few days. I thought that I would have to think about some sunscreen cream but it is expensive and I told myself that it wouldn't matter for a short time but this is silly realty out in the garden as l am in all day. The cushion was in a chair in the strong sunlight from the window so I moved it away so that the colour wouldn't fade. When it caught my eye again it was sort of creased and so the face had wrinkles. In the pound shop was Protection Sun cream, so I remembered the wrinkled little face and bought it, knowing, from past experience, that I ignore their advice at my peril.

Come to think of it, what did I do with that dress? I never got to wear it; in a box all those years. I remember now, I dyed it green, it took the dye beautifully and it was worn by a little guest at CINDERELLA'S BALL!

You've got to hand it to them, haven't you? Those kids have got some good ideas. They have since pointed out that when they reach college age as they do, they no longer wish to be called kids, instead they are no longer `kids' but LIFEGUARDS! But how l know that is another story.

The day after I had recorded this, I noticed in a shop window gorgeous models of Disney characters CINDERELLA and SNOW-WHITE I noticed that the reproduction was perfect. So many of them have not captured the character that is so important in the original pictures but these new ones are perfect Very expensive but lovely. Inside the shop there was a video with the original design on the case that in subsequent editions is not as accurate so I bought it. NANCY had been attracting my attention all that morning but to try to write it all down would take too much space. The theme was repeated with other instances so they are saying something. I think it could be, the original book THERE'S A RAINBOW ON THE RIVER was charming but the next publisher will be "the real thing".

On the same shelf was a little box and its title HOW TO MAKE NINETEEN KITES!

The little ones have since said that they want to be called LIFE GUARDS too. After all they do see me over the road and are always finding my specs.

I shall be eternally grateful to Austin Macauley publishers for transferring my manuscript into book form. When the editor rang me to say that they wished to publish it, her words were people everywhere need this. I think she will be glad that it didn't end up in a recycling bin. I shall keep her in touch (If she is still with them) about what happened to it.

Within three days I counted FIVE CAROUSELS. I had a job to decipher the reason for those so I asked them to explain. Sure enough, on came the delightful programme ESCAPE TO THE CHÂTEAU and the lovely ANGEL refers to a `MERRY GO ROUND'. The expression I had used in the prologue, where I had described the unfortunate effect of the adverse MERRY GO ROUND so l wasn't comforted until I noticed that they had MIRRORS in the centre. The unhappy MERRY GO ROUND has started to REVERSE. The backlog reaction is beginning to bum out now that a lot of people are beginning to get used to it just as they had promised at the beginning of this experience.

This year when the BRIGADOON anniversary came

round, no reminder of the lovely day occurred. I was puzzled, in all that time the date was never allowed to pass without some reference to remind me during that week in October. It was at least ten days after that to my astonishment one morning the oblong of light came up on the PICTURE of JESUS knocking on the door. They must have worked out the angle of the sun and the weather knowing that there was a good chance of it appearing for the third time in all those years. Each day BELLS began to RING followed by a CHIMING CLOCK, sometimes the other what round unfailingly, as they had done before. Soon after RACE HORSES getting near the winning post and SAILING SHIPS in harbour and a remark in a repeated AD: (Call the midwife) Room for one more?

The tip off to send the book again to a new publisher did materialize, just as they had said it would, with `Look out for THUNDERBIRDS' the filmed puppet series. Sure enough up it came. This time though it was acted by real people (THE REAL THING?) and the last words of the dialogue was `The world needs THUNDERBIRDS and THUNDERBIRDS need the world' (International Rescue) echoing the words I had included in my pre written letter to the new publisher.

They also saw to it that I should switch on at the beginning of a film called `IN WHICH WE SERVE', a film of a ship. Noel Coward who produced it had the idea to use real sailors in action scenes and my brother was one of them. He and his friends had manned the POM POM guns that are portrayed in the film in the REAL action (Note the `real thing' again). His invisible guardians must have had a worrying time keeping him safe. In spite of the cruiser HMS LIVERPOOL having been torpedoed leaving her with seventy feet just hanging off her end against all odds she limped into harbour.

The term THE REAL THING came up consistently, followed by more stories of determination and survival and close shaves, against all odds like the film THE FLIGHT OF THE PHOENIX., THE MEMPHIS BELLE, THE FIRST OF THE FEW, the story of the SPITFIRE and the one that sums up the struggle on the part of the Dimension people to get this knowledge to us before its evolutionary time most, I think was APOLLO 13 when the spaceship crew got stuck and the NASA people had to use the almost impossible ingenuity to get them down safely. It reminded me too of the plane that must have only got down in time that day. The point being that no matter how difficult it will be, we will with their guidance be successful in combating the problems that the world has to face and in the end no matter how difficult or how long it takes, WE ARE IN TIME and all in the end will be well.

In my Gmail were advertisements for early booking for flower shows. I didn't take any notice and deleted them. Garden programmes are continually coming up on the telly so often and I didn't pay any attention to them either, forgetting that we must always check out repetition. The funny programme KEEPING UP APPEARANCES was shown once again with HYACINTH getting in a right muddle by trying to turn her house into a conservatory of very posh plants. Someone mentioned a RUBBER TREE PLANT and the GREENHOUSE EFFECT. ROSE and DAISY had the last laugh as usual and I began to notice when KEYS came up day after day.

Within a very few days I have been once again frequently reminded of BEE's, the delightful programme

TO THE MANOR BORN, with the class conscious lady who is very aware of her status and is very funny, becomes interested in BEE'S & wasn't till the subject came up over and over again that I realised that they are on about their BEE'S again. References to BEEHIVES coming up several times in a short time. In the SUBWAY line-up a young man in front of me had written on his TEE shirt BUZZ for instance. So, I was puzzled. They are saying SOMETHING that's for sure, with a reference to the up-market store in LONDON where they keep bees on the roof and pictures of the lovely gardens that surround it. A success story of their concern for the environment. Hence my attention is so frequently drawn again to advertisements to sow wild flower seeds to encourage BUSY BEES and to ALL HANDS ON DECK

Would you believe it? When I had finished this I felt strained and worried in case I had made a hash of it, miserably aware of my lack of typing skills.

I put the telly on and immediately a fleet of B17's are flying across the sky and the dialogue of a veteran from the US Air force "no use dwelling on it"

In other words, you've done your best even though you found it a `fight,' now forget and go into the garden and relax and leave the rest to the BEES!

Like ALEX said "CLEVER STUFF ISN'T IT!", but before I go.......

When I was in Oxford street in London, I saw a pair of Jeans in a shop window with the price tag of ten pounds They had holes in the knees and were called distressed! And at that time push chairs became so big that it was a major operation to get them on a bus the examples of the tendency for designing in all sorts of areas a bit `cock-eyed'

226

as the saying goes. People didn't seem to notice it. I used to think that when prams and push chairs became sensible then the beginning of the end of this era of transition when people can be more rational would begin. That was a long time ago but before long there will be signs of recovery. When out shopping last week I saw, in a charity shop, a young mother pushing a lovely little pram. Compact comfortable and easy to get on a bus. Instantly two more exactly the same except different colours so Mums will have a choice. The designs which were sensible but ugly or elegant but impractical are beginning to change. Not only the little Silver Cross pram has leaped forward in design I see that other makes are following suit and charming appearance combined with practicability is replacing the ugly oversize wheels that has been so predominant.

Sales may well fall of sugary stuff too when people gain confidence in the future but there is no need to fear for businesses as nothing can change quickly. This is just one area that the Dimension are working on to come up with the answers when the changes do come. Only an intelligence of outstanding order could find a way out because of the "knock on effect" in time everyone will have peace of mind AND SO ALL WILL BE ABLE TO BE RECEPTIVE TO THE GUIDANCE THAT WILL STEER THEM TOWARDS ALTERNATIVE SOLUTIONS.

My typing skills never improved towards the end of the book. I was still struggling with a world that was out of my province. At one point I was afraid that I would not be able to complete the task that had been assigned to me.

A film came up called D Day 6th of June AND featured a young actor who was actually part of the `real thing' and the events were covered exactly as ALEX had related, where they had reached a point where their supplies and rations were running out dangerously.

Their orders had been…. WAIT UNTIL RELIEVED!

Alarmingly close to disaster when they heard BAGPIPES! A Scottish division was on its way to relieve them.

I should have known that somehow rescue would come, and it did in the form of a beautiful young man who was experienced in the world of computers and compassionate enough to give hours of his time to rescue me.

No wonder I was getting Bagpipes every time I put the telly on!

I think the time is not far away now, when others will hear

THE BAGPIPES OF BRIGADOON

COPYRIGHT ACKNOWLEDGEMENTS